Nelly the Monster Sitter

KT-415-338

Copyright © 2008 Kes Gray
Illustrations copyright © 2008 Stephen Hanson

First published in Great Britain in 2008
by Hodder Children's Books

The right of Kes Gray and Stephen Hanson to be identified as the Author and Illustrator of the Work respectively have been asserted by them in accordance with the Copyright, Designs and Patents Act 1988.

1

All rights reserved. Apart from any use permitted under UK copyright law, this publication may only be reproduced, stored or transmitted, in any form, or by any means with prior permission in writing from the publishers or in the case of reprographic production in accordance with the terms of licences issued by the Copyright Licensing Agency and may not be otherwise circulated in any form of binding or cover other than that in which it is published and without a similar condition being imposed on the subsequent purchaser.

All characters in this publication are fictitious and any resemblance to real persons, living or dead, is purely coincidental.

A Catalogue record for this book is available from the British Library

ISBN 978 0 340 93192 9

Typeset in NewBaskerville by Avon DataSet Ltd,
Bidford on Avon, Warwickshire

Printed and bound in Great Britain by
CPI Bookmarque, Croydon, CR0 4TD

The paper and board used in this paperback by Hodder Children's Books are natural recyclable products made from wood grown in sustainable forests. The manufacturing processes conform to the environmental regulations of the country of origin.

Hodder Children's Books
a division of Hachette Children's Books
338 Euston Road, London NW1 3BH
An Hachette Livre UK company

Nelly the Monster Sitter

Ultravores, Rimes & Watt Watts

KES GRAY

Illustrated by Stephen Hanson

A division of Hachette Children's Books

Read more about Nelly the Monster Sitter
in these other titles

Grerks, Squurms and Water Greeps
Cowcumbers, Pipplewaks and Altigators
Huffaluks, Muggots and Thermitts
Polarbores, Digdiggs and Dendrilegs

NELLY THE MONSTER SITTER

'If monsters are real, how come I've never seen one?' said Nelly.

'Because they never go out,' said her dad.

'Why don't monsters ever go out?' said Nelly.

'Because they can never get a baby sitter,' said her dad.

Nelly thought about it. Her mum and dad never went out unless they could get a baby sitter. Why should monsters be any different?

'Then I shall become Nelly the Monster Sitter!' smiled Nelly.

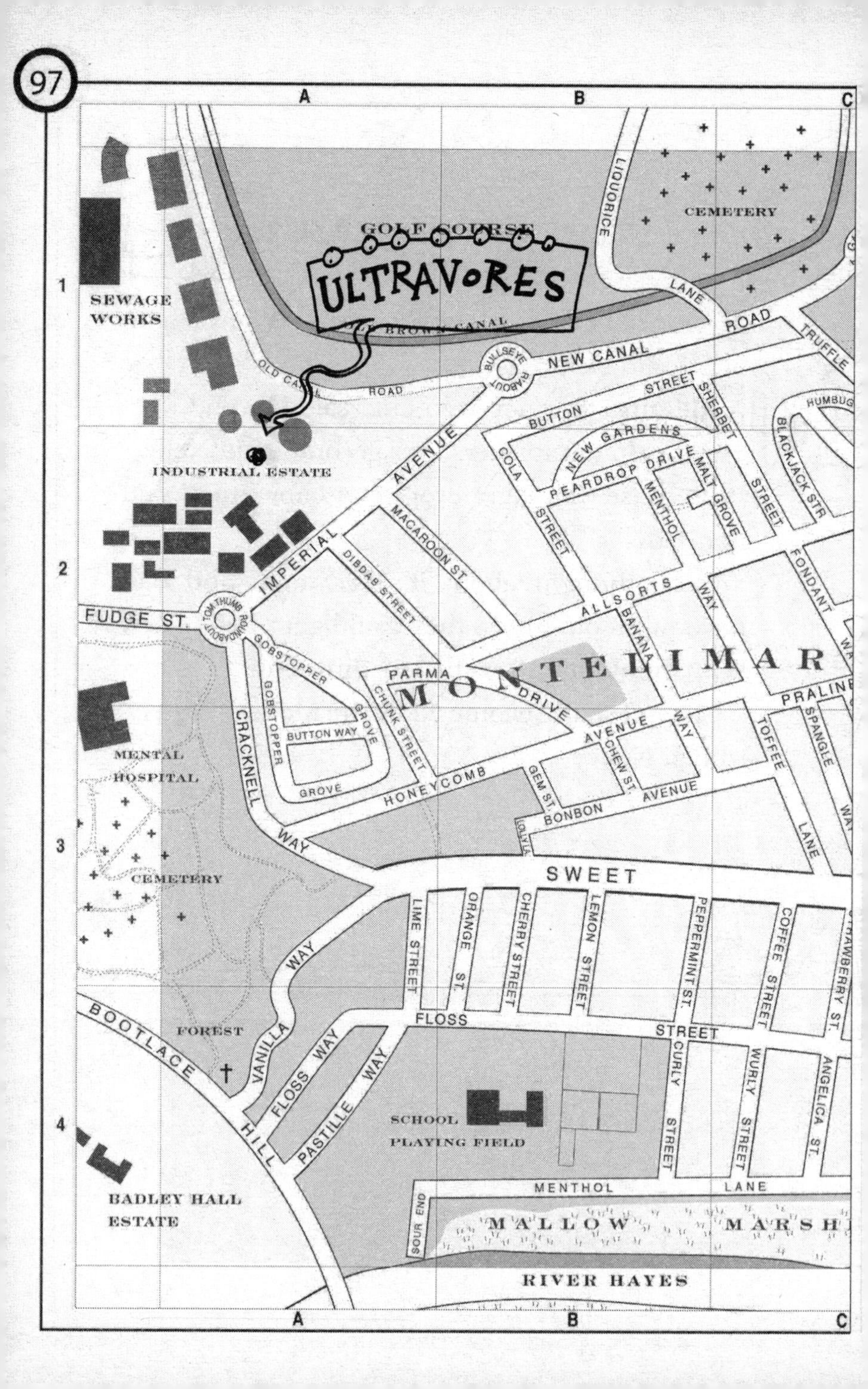
ULTRAVORES
GOLF COURSE
SEWAGE WORKS
INDUSTRIAL ESTATE
CEMETERY
LIQUORICE LANE
NEW CANAL ROAD
BULLSEYE R'ABOUT
OLD CANAL ROAD
TRUFFLE
HUMBUG
BUTTON STREET
SHERBET STREET
NEW GARDENS
PEARDROP DRIVE
COLA STREET
MALT GROVE
MENTHOL
BLACKJACK STR
IMPERIAL AVENUE
MACAROON ST.
DIBDAB STREET
ALLSORTS WAY
BANANA
FONDANT
FUDGE ST.
TOM THUMB ROUNDABOUT
GOBSTOPPER GROVE
GOBSTOPPER
BUTTON WAY
GROVE
MONTELIMAR
PARMA DRIVE
CHUNK STREET
PRALINE
CRACKNELL WAY
AVENUE
CHEW ST.
WAY
TOFFEE LANE
SPANGLE
HONEYCOMB
GEM ST.
BONBON AVENUE
LOLLY
MENTAL HOSPITAL
CEMETERY
SWEET
LIME STREET
ORANGE ST.
CHERRY STREET
LEMON STREET
PEPPERMINT ST.
COFFEE STREET
STRAWBERRY ST.
VANILLA WAY
FLOSS STREET
FLOSS WAY
PASTILLE WAY
BOOTLACE HILL
FOREST
CURLY STREET
WURLY STREET
ANGELICA ST.
SCHOOL
PLAYING FIELD
BADLEY HALL ESTATE
MENTHOL LANE
SOUR END
MALLOW MARSH
RIVER HAYES

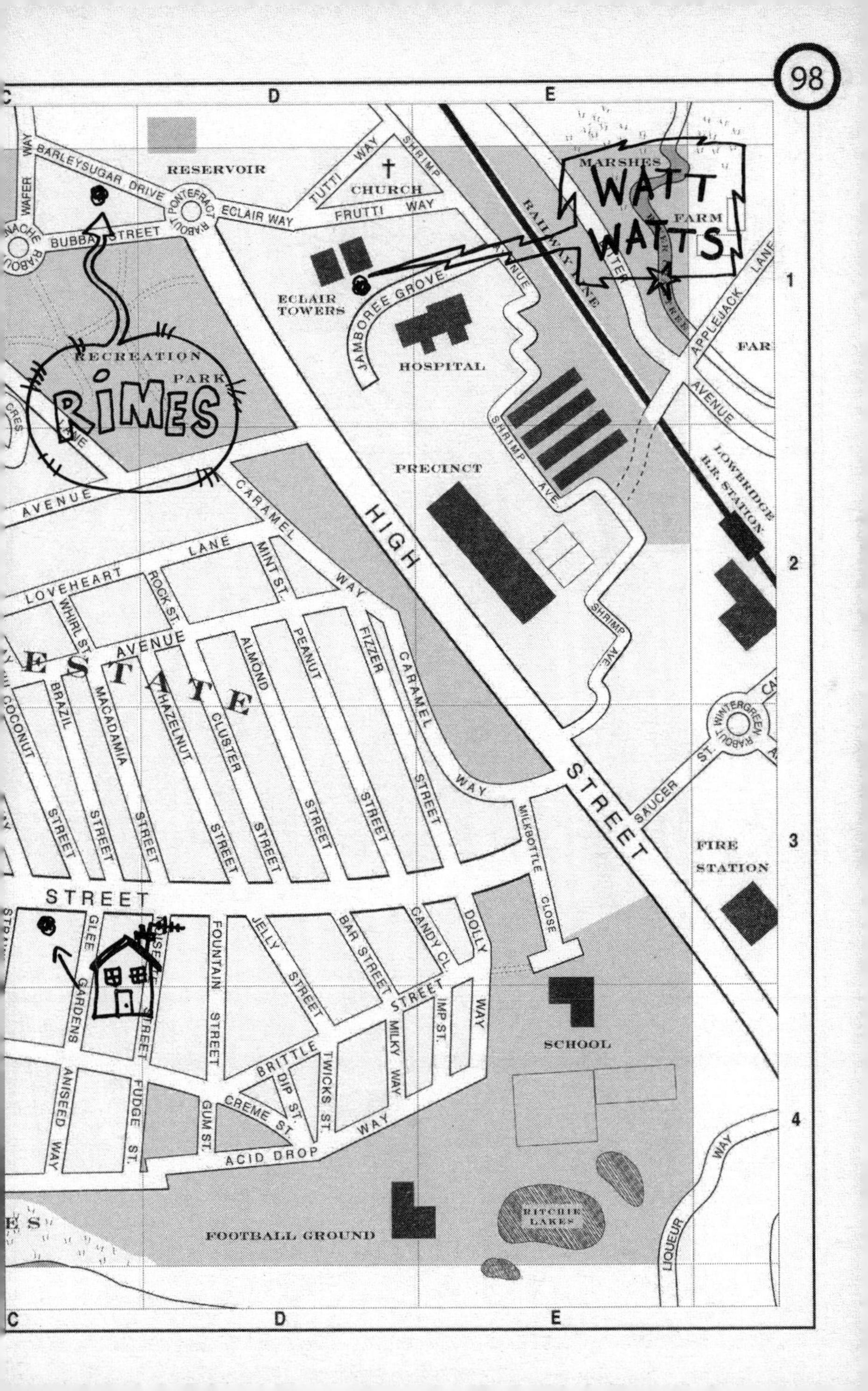

RESERVOIR
BARLEYSUGAR DRIVE
WAFER WAY
PONTEFRACT R'ABOUT
ECLAIR WAY
BUBBA STREET
TUTTI WAY
CHURCH
FRUTTI WAY
SHRIMP
MARSHES
WATT WATTS
FARM
RAILWAY LANE
ECLAIR TOWERS
JAMBOREE GROVE
HOSPITAL
APPLEJACK LANE
AVENUE
RECREATION PARK
RIMES
PRECINCT
SHRIMP AVE
LOWBRIDGE R.R. STATION
AVENUE
CARAMEL WAY
HIGH STREET
LANE
LOVEHEART
ROCK ST.
MINT ST.
WHIRL ST.
AVENUE
ESTATE
COCONUT STREET
BRAZIL STREET
MACADAMIA STREET
HAZELNUT STREET
CLUSTER STREET
ALMOND STREET
PEANUT STREET
FIZZER STREET
CARAMEL STREET
WINTERGREEN R'ABOUT
SAUCER ST.
MILKBOTTLE CLOSE
FIRE STATION
STREET
GLEE GARDENS
FOUNTAIN STREET
JELLY STREET
BAR STREET
CANDY CL.
DOLLY WAY
STREET
IMP ST.
MILKY WAY
SCHOOL
BRITTLE
TWICKS ST.
DIP ST.
ANISEED WAY
FUDGE ST.
GUM ST.
CREME ST.
WAY
ACID DROP
RITCHIE LAKES
LIQUEUR WAY
FOOTBALL GROUND
C D E
1 2 3 4

THE
ULTRAVORES
AT NO. 11

1

'Have you seen an African grey parrot anywhere?' said Nelly, lobbing her school bag towards the bottom of the stairs and then kicking her school shoes somewhere in the general direction of the lounge.

Nelly's mum looked up from her Sudoku, removed a pencil from her mouth and lobbed a puzzled glance back from the kitchen.

'Have I seen a what?' she asked.

'An African grey parrot,' said Nelly, screwing her school tie into a ball and stuffing it into the pocket of her blazer. 'Someone in Fountain Street has lost a pet parrot called Fevvers. They've stuck notices on the lamp posts all the way up the road.'

'Serves them right for keeping a pet parrot in the first place,' said Nelly's mum, turning her pencil upside down and then erasing a number seven with a frown. 'Birds aren't meant to be pets, and they're not meant to be kept in cages, it's cruel. Parrots are meant to fly free, not sit on a perch and squawk "*who's a pretty boy, who's a pretty boy, who's a pretty boy*" all day.'

Nelly hovered halfway between the hallway and the lounge. She had no idea her mum was so birdy aware.

'I suppose you're right,' agreed Nelly, 'but there's a two-hundred-pound reward if I can find it.'

'Blood money,' said Nelly's mum, cartwheeling her pencil the right way up, and replacing the number seven with a number four.

'I could do a lot with two hundred pounds,' thought Nelly, leaving the hallway and heading in the direction of the TV remote. 'I could do a lot with TWENTY pounds even!'

'Can I have my belly button pierced?' said Asti, bursting in through the open front door, lobbing her school bag at the radiator and then throwing a venomous glance at Nelly.

'No you can't,' said Nelly's mum with unblinking firmness.

The shoulders of Asti's school blazer slumped. 'Why not?' she protested. 'I'm nearly thirteen years old! And I'll pay for it out of my own money. I've still got loads of money saved up from Christmas.'

Nelly's mum ran the tip of her pencil down another Sudoku column and then triumphantly added the number two to another square.

'Well, can I get my nose pierced then?' said Asti, stamping her school shoes into the carpet. 'Or my tongue?'

'No, you can't,' said Nelly's mum, with the quiet but firm authority of a snooker referee.

'Why don't you get your head pierced?' shouted Nelly from the settee. 'With a javelin! There's plenty in the gym cupboard at school!'

Asti wrenched her blazer from her shoulders and spun round. 'And why don't you stick your head in a bucket of wet cement and leave it there till it sets, you freak lover!'

'Temper temper!' grinned Nelly, raising the

TV remote and skipping through the programme menu on offer.

'I'm going to ask Dad when he gets home,' hissed Asti, sending a volley of disdainful glances in two directions at once, kicking the front door closed and then stomping upstairs to her room.

'I bet Dad'll let me!' she shouted, with a slam of her bedroom door.

'I bet he won't,' smiled Nelly.

2

'Have you seen an African grey parrot!' shouted Nelly, the instant her dad arrived home from work.

'Can I have my belly button pierced?' blurted Asti, racing down the stairs and nailing her dad to the front door with pleading eyes.

Dad gulped, sidled nervously towards the coat hooks and slowly removed his jacket.

'Someone in Fountain Street has lost a pet parrot called Fevvers,' gasped Nelly leaping up from the settee and charging into the hallway. 'There's a two-hundred-pound reward if we can find it!'

'I REALLY want to get my belly button pierced,' pleaded Asti. 'I'll pay for it with my own money and everything!' she begged. 'PLEASE, Dad, can I get my belly button pierced, can I???'

Dad sighed and then angled his head forlornly back in the direction of the coat hooks. He had walked into a domestic tornado. The best thing surely would be to just slip his jacket back on and go back to work.

'DID you see a parrot on the way home from work?' pressed Nelly.

'I'm nearly thirteen, Dad, I'm old enough to do anything I want!' urged Asti.

'Hi, honey, I'm home!' said Dad, sidestepping around both of his daughters and making a break for the kitchen. 'What's for dinner?'

Mum swept some pencil erasings away from her newspaper with the back of her hand and then added the number six to her Sudoku.

'I haven't really thought about it, Clifford,' she mumbled. 'I've been really busy. Have you had a good day?'

Dad shuffled into the kitchen, shadowed by both of his daughters.

'Would anyone like a cup of tea?' he asked, lifting the lid of the kettle to check there was enough water inside. 'Don't worry, I'll make it.'

'HAVE you seen a parrot, Dad?' asked Nelly with a nod of her head.

'CAN I have my belly button pierced?' pleaded Asti with a nod of hers.

There were times when Clifford T. Morton, chief provider for the Morton household, senior draughtsman at Sandleys Engineering and principal tea maker at both, really did feel compelled to ask himself, just what was his life actually all about?

This was one of those times.

No sooner had he stepped through the door of his own home after a long and tedious day at work than he had been blown off his feet by a whirlwind of belly buttons and parrots. There had been no welcome when he arrived home, no dinner on the table, no dinner even planned. There was just belly buttons and parrots.

'NO!' he said wearily, prodding the kettle switch with his finger, and then plopping a tea bag into his favourite mug. 'NO I haven't seen a parrot and no you can't have your belly button pierced.'

Nelly sighed, and turned back in the direction of the lounge.

Asti exploded.

'WHY NOT?' she screamed. 'I'm nearly THIRTEEN!' She shook. 'It's my money, It's my belly button, I'm not a kid, I'M NEARLY THIRTEEN!'

There was a soft thud as the girls' mum dropped her pencil on to the kitchen table, screwed the puzzle page of her newspaper into a ball and then fixed Asti with a glare. Unfortunately for Asti, the Sudoku hadn't gone well.

'If you're nearly thirteen, Astilbe, then I suggest you stop acting like you're nearly two. If God had intended you to be full of holes then you would have come into this world as a colander or a pair of your dad's socks. You may think *nearly* thirteen is a responsible age to be making decisions about puncturing your body, but your father and I do not. Belly-button piercing is not only a barbaric form of self-abuse, it also carries the risk of septicaemia. Do you know what septicaemia is, young lady? Well, before you try and tell me, let me tell you. It's another word for blood poisoning. If your belly-button piercing becomes infected then you could get an infection and that infection could lead to blood poisoning. Is that what you want? No, it isn't what your father and I want for you either. So no, you cannot have your belly button pierced, either with your own money or a loan from the governor of the Bank of England. And the same goes for your tongue and your nose and any other part of your body you might care to stick a sharp object in!'

Asti's jaw dropped, and then her face turned puce with frustration.

'Apart from your ears,' added Nelly, a little taken aback by the ferocity of her mum's outburst.

'I've already got my ears pierced!' squealed Asti. 'And so have you! We had our ears pierced years ago!'

'Ears are different,' growled her mum.

'WHY ARE THEY DIFFERENT?' squawked Asti.

'Because they are,' replied her mum in an

infuriatingly under-explained way.

Dad stared wearily into his mug as his tea bag depth-charged out of view. First it had been parrots, then it had been belly buttons, now it was tongues, noses and septicaemia. He really should have stayed at work.

'Astilbe love, why do you want to fill yourself full of holes anyway?' he asked, trying to adopt the role of peacekeeper. 'You're beautiful just the way you are.'

'It's not filling myself full of holes, it's belly-button piercing!' screeched Asti.

'She wants to look cool at the school disco,' said Nelly.

'I DO NOT!' screamed Asti.

'YES YOU DO!' shouted Nelly. 'You've been wanging on about it all week. You fancy Darren Leadbetter and you think if you get your belly button pierced he'll think you're really cool.'

'YES, well YOUUUU fancy Craig Parmenter,' countered Asti.

'So what if I do,' said Nelly. 'It doesn't mean I'd fill myself full of holes just to make him like me.'

'I don't know why he likes you anyway!' sneered Asti. 'Look at the clothes you wear, look at the trainers you wear. You don't even wear make-up! You don't even eat CRISPBREADS!'

'So?' said Nelly indifferently.

'Soooo . . .' stammered Asti, 'soooo . . . you're a pasty-faced, monster-loving, embarrassing uncool fashion disaster of a sister, Nelly Morton, and I hate you!'

'And you're not allowed to get your belly button pierced!' said Nelly, turning with a smirk and marching back to the settee.

'Takeaway for dinner?' sighed Dad, with a slurp.

'Good idea,' frowned Mum. 'And yes I would like a cup of tea, Clifford.'

3

When Nelly left for school the next morning, she stepped out of the house armed with a small notebook and pen. She had spent the night thinking about all the things she could do with two hundred pounds and had resolved to write down the telephone number of the person who had lost the parrot.

But that wasn't all. Ever resourceful, and ever open to bigger and more ambitious ideas, Nelly had decided to start her own company. It was going to be a lost-pet-finding company, and it was going to be called . . . well, she wasn't sure what it was going to be called yet, but it was going to make her lots of money.

When Asti left for school that morning she stomped out of the house with a face like poisoned porridge. She had spent the entire

night thinking about all the places she would like to stab her family with a belly-button piercer and had resolved to spend all her Christmas money on hiring a hit man to take them out.

The two sisters walked separately to school and returned home separately at the end of the day.

'I'll call it LostandHound.com!' smiled Nelly, swinging her school bag down from her shoulder, and then retrieving her notebook from a jumble of exercise books, textbooks and pens.

She stopped in the middle of the pavement for a moment and opened the notebook at the parrot page.

'Mmmm,' she frowned. 'Hounds doesn't really include parrots . . . or cats.'

She frowned again. 'Lost and Hound is a good name though . . . maybe I could only find lost dogs?'

She nibbled the top of her pen, and then agonized a little further. 'But if I only find lost dogs, the rewards might not be so big. Plus I might find a lost cat when I'm looking for a lost dog. Then what would I do?'

'You're dead,' hissed Asti, stomping past her with a scowl.

'You're sad,' smiled Nelly, closing the

notebook and then opening it again with a whoop of excitement.

'Pets Reunited! That's what I'll call it! I'll call it PetsReunited.com, that way I'll be able to find any kind of pet that I want! Pets Reunited it is!'

Nelly swung her school bag back on to her shoulder and hurried home to get cracking.

She overtook Asti as she turned into Sweet Street but was too engrossed in thoughts of corporate identity to even hear the names her sister called her as she passed.

'I'm going to need to design a business card,' she thought as she turned the key in the front door. 'I'm going to need a website,' she thought, as she kicked her shoes in the direction of the lounge, 'and an advertising campaign, leaflets and everything.'

'Maybe I could go on telly to tell everyone about it,' she thought as she ran up the stairs to her room. 'Maybe I could do a national TV launch!'

Nelly closed the door of her bedroom and settled down at her homework desk. After appointing herself Chairman, Managing Director and Chief Executive Officer of her own company, she set about awarding herself a salary of about a million pounds a year.

After appointing herself Executive Creative Director too, she set about designing her business card.

It was only after appointing herself Chief Finance Director that it suddenly dawned on her that she didn't have any of the money that she would need to pay for business card printing, website and advertising launches, or even lost-pet-bait, like doggy chews, balls of wool and sunflower seeds.

'Actually,' Nelly thought, leaning back in her director's chair and placing her socks on the boardroom table, 'I probably don't need all that stuff. It's probably better if I start small, just go out on my bike and look for lamp posts with lost-pet notices on them, and write the telephone numbers down. I could try the vets' too. There are always lost pets advertised in the vets'. I could stick a Pets Reunited poster on the noticeboard!'

And that's precisely what Nelly did. Over the

following week, after school, Nelly scoured the streets of the Montelimar Estate, looking for lamp posts and telegraph poles with lost-pet notices attached to them. She placed her own notice in the vets' too and after four days of Pets Reunited launch work and legwork, she had added a lost tabby cat and a runaway chocolate Labrador to her notebook.

The tabby cat was called Shelley, and had been lost by an owner who lived in Button Way. The reward being offered was ten pounds.

The chocolate Labrador was called Benson, and had been lost by a publican in the high street. The reward being offered was 'all the beer you can drink in one evening. Spirits not included'.

That was it. Nelly had one parrot and a cat to look for, and two hundred and ten pounds reward money to earn. (She had decided to pass on the chocolate Labrador. Beer wasn't really her thing.)

One week later, she still only had one parrot and a tabby cat to look for. Her feet ached from walking the streets, her neck ached from scouring the sky and her hand ached from drawing more posters.

With a shrug and a sigh she flopped on to her bed and dissolved her pet-finding company there and then.

'Oh well,' she sighed, 'the reward money would have been handy. But I'm far too busy to look for pets anyway.'

With the accuracy of a professional dart-thrower she united her Pets Reunited notebook with the litter bin in her bedroom.

'Anyway, if my pet-finding company had taken off, I wouldn't have had any time to do my monster sitting. Monster sitting is much more fun!'

She turned towards the desk in her bedroom and opened her monster sitting diary.

Thoughts of tabby cats, parrots and chocolate Labradors evaporated in an instant. She had almost forgotten. She had a new family of monsters to visit! They lived near Imperial Avenue and were pencilled into her diary for this coming weekend.

Nelly traced over the date and time with her strawberry gel pen and then underlined the monster family's name and address with a smile.

'Much MUCH more fun than looking for lost pets!' she smiled.

They were the Ultravores at Unit 11!

4

When Saturday arrived, Nelly sprang from her bed like a gazelle.

At around 4.30 in the afternoon, after begging her dad for a lift all day, Nelly set off in the Maestro in the direction of Imperial Avenue.

'Can you believe it?' said her dad, turning the car out of Sweet Street. 'The ambulance drivers have gone on strike!'

Nelly turned to her dad and shrugged. She wasn't sure how to reply to that one.

'I was driving home from work yesterday along Shrimp Avenue,' continued her dad. 'I was just passing the entrance to the hospital, and guess what I saw?'

'Striking ambulance drivers?' guessed Nelly.

'Precisely,' puffed her dad. 'A whole gang of striking ambulance drivers, holding up a big

banner that read, "TOOT IF YOU SUPPORT THE AMBULANCE DRIVERS."'

'Did you toot?' asked Nelly.

'NO I DID NOT TOOT!' exclaimed her dad. 'What if there's an emergency? What if there's a car crash or something, and someone needs an ambulance? If all the ambulance drivers are on strike, there won't be anyone to assist, will there! It's an absolute outrage,' he said, indicating right as the Maestro approached Cracknell Way.

'Why are they striking?' asked Nelly, keen to get both sides of the story.

'More money,' he sighed. 'Everyone always wants more money. *I'd* like more money, but I don't go on strike every time I want it.'

'*I'd* like some more money too,' thought Nelly, glancing at the lamp posts that lined her side of the road.

'Are we still looking out for parrots and lost-pet notices?' asked her dad, guessing that their route to the Ultravores might take Nelly past some lamp posts and telegraph poles that she hadn't scrutinized before.

Nelly shook her head and rather belatedly clicked her seat belt into position. 'I'm not looking for lost pets any more,' she said, 'and anyway, Fevvers has probably reached the Amazon by now.'

Nelly's dad flicked his eyes from the road ahead to Nelly's fingers as they finished their fumble with the seat belt clasp.

'I've told you before about fastening your seat belt after the car has started,' he frowned. 'You're supposed to put your belt on before the car pulls away, not a mile down the road.'

'Sorry, Dad,' said Nelly. 'I forgot.'

'Well, don't forget!' said her dad, dropping down to third gear, and then steering the topic of conversation back in the direction of pet rescue. 'You know Wilbury Safari Park lost a sea lion last year.'

'You're kidding!' laughed Nelly.

'I'm not,' said Nelly's dad. 'It escaped down the river that flows through the estate. It went through a gap in the fence, down a sluice and out into freedom.'

'Did they catch it?' asked Nelly.

'I've no idea!' chuckled Nelly's dad. It was on a documentary I was watching. They hadn't caught it when the documentary was being made.'

'I wonder what the reward money was for that!' laughed Nelly.

'More than a parrot!' chuckled her dad.

'Hey, I bet I know what the documentary was called,' chuckled Nelly.

'Go on then,' smiled her dad.

'*Seal Or No Seal*!' laughed Nelly.

'You're not meant to laugh at your own jokes,' tutted her dad.

'I couldn't help it,' apologized Nelly.

Nelly smiled again and peered past her dad in the direction of Parma Drive. Her good friends the Cowcumbers lived just three or four roads away.

'You know, if you want to earn some extra pocket money, Nelly,' said her dad, 'you should think about charging for all this monster sitting you keep doing. How many different monster families are you babysitting for now?'

'About twenty-five,' shrugged Nelly, 'but I'm not going to charge them money to do it. I do it for the fun, not the money. And to help them out.'

'I don't remember you having much fun at the Digdiggs,' said her dad, dropping down another gear on the approach to the Tom Thumb roundabout.

'That was a different type of fun,' said Nelly.

'It sounded serious to me.'

'Call it serious fun then!' smiled Nelly. 'That's what makes monster sitting so fantastic. I never know who I'm going to meet or what is going to happen.'

'Sounds scary to me,' said her dad, taking the second exit off the roundabout into Imperial Avenue.

'Anyway,' said Nelly, 'I don't know if monsters even use money. I have no idea what they use to buy things, or IF they even buy things. Maybe monsters do things differently to us.'

'Maybe,' nodded her dad, slowing the car in anticipation of a hand signal from Nelly.

'Do these Ultravores actually live in a house on Imperial Avenue?' he asked. 'I don't think I'd like to live on a busy main road like this.'

Nelly switched her interest to the kerb side of the road and pointed a hundred metres further ahead.

'They live in a unit on the industrial estate,' she explained. 'Turn in through the main entrance, it's Unit number 11.'

'Unit number 11?' chuckled her dad. 'That's a

strange address to have. These Ultravores sound like a peculiar bunch to me.'

Nelly smiled. 'They sounded ultra friendly on the phone!' she laughed.

'Then I shall be on my ultra best behaviour when I meet them!' smiled her dad.

Nelly prodded the air with her left finger and then relaxed back into her seat as her dad flicked the indicator.

'Ultravores, here I come!' smiled Nelly as the Maestro turned off the main road and then ground to an immediate halt.

The entrance to the industrial estate was barred by an automatic barrier. It remained barred for some moments as Nelly's dad tried to attract the attention of the security guard that was sitting alone in the sentry box stationed alongside the barrier.

Far from being on duty, he seemed to be more than a little preoccupied with the music he was listening to on his iPod, plus the football results that he was simultaneously watching on a small black and white portable TV.

Nelly's dad unclipped his seat belt with a sigh, and opened the door of the car.

The security man jumped out of his skin as Nelly's dad's arm reached in through the window of the box and tapped him on his back.

'Sorry guv'nor!' he blustered. 'We don't get much traffic through 'ere on a Saturday, specially not this late in the day. What can I do you for?'

'Unit 11, please,' said Nelly's dad. 'Can you point me in the right direction?'

The security guard pulled a clipboard out from under his newspaper and then ran his finger across the site map.

He ran his finger across again, and then once more and again and again.

'Are you sure you mean Unit 11?' he asked, craning his head forward in the direction of the Maestro.

Nelly waved back with a smile.

Nelly's dad turned towards the car and double-checked.

'Are we sure we want Unit 11, Nelly?' he shouted.

Nelly gave a double thumbs-up and grinned.

'We're positive!' smiled Nelly's dad. 'My daughter's doing a spot of mon . . . I mean babysitting for the family that lives there.'

The security guard swallowed drily, and rasped his chin with the palm of his hand.

'There's a family living in there, is there?' he drawled. 'I ain't never seen no family livin' there.'

'That's because they never go out,' explained Nelly's dad.

'All I seen comin' from in there is strange lights. Bright lights . . .' whispered the security guard.

'Well, they've never been able to go out until now,' expanded Nelly's dad. 'That's what my daughter does, you see, she babysits for parents who have never had the opportunity to go out and enjoy themselves.'

The security guard's eyebrows arched like startled caterpillars and then dropped in the direction of the clipboard.

'Are you sure you want Unit 11?' he whispered.

'We're sure,' sighed Nelly's dad, starting to tire of the amateur dramatics.

'Straight down, first right, second left,' said the security guard, raising the barrier with a press of a button, and then turning back to his portable TV to catch the results of the late kickoffs.

'What a weirdo,' puffed Nelly's dad, clicking his seat belt back into position and steering the Maestro through the barriers and on to the industrial estate.

'What did he say?' asked Nelly.

'First right, second left,' replied her dad.

'No, I mean what did he say about the Ultravores?' asked Nelly.

'Nothing much,' said Nelly's dad with a shrug. 'All he went on about was strange lights.'

5

There were no strange lights as far as Nelly and her dad could see, as they pulled up in the car outside Unit 11.

There was just an industrial unit that looked much the same as all the other units on the industrial estate.

The Ultravores' home looked a bit like a box in fact. Built from ribbed steel sheeting and studded with galvanized rivets, it was grey-blue in colour, rectangular in shape, and perhaps twice the width of Nelly's house.

Its windows were different to the neighbouring units. Instead of being high, narrow and security-grilled, they were wide, deep and rectangular. There were two windows at the front of the unit, glazed black for maximum privacy, and polished bright for maximum shine.

'The windows are like limousine glass!' thought Nelly, as she unclipped her seat belt excitedly and tumbled from the car.

'Very mod!' said Nelly's dad, removing the car keys from the ignition, and opening his driver door.

'Here I go!' smiled Nelly, determined to be first to ring the doorbell.

Except there was no doorbell. The Ultravores' front door had no features whatsoever. No bell, no letter box, no door knocker, no house number, no front step, no nothing. In fact it was nothing more than a sheet of glittering black glass.

Nelly dropped her doorbell-ringing finger by her side and frowned at her dad.

'Do you think we should just knock on the glass instead?' she asked.

Nelly's dad shook his head slowly and then urgently redirected her eyes back towards the door.

Nelly turned and gulped. The sheet of black glass in front of them was no longer black and impenetrable, it was as transparent as the air itself!

It was still very much there though, for as Nelly raised her arm instinctively to shake the hand of the Ultravore standing behind it, her knuckles rapped sharply against the surface.

'Ooops!' thought Nelly, smiling through the glass at the monster standing before them. 'Silly me!'

The broad and cavernous smile of huge toad-faced head grinned widely back at them through the transparent door as Nelly withdrew her knuckle with a wince.

'He looks a bit weird,' whispered her dad out of the corner of his mouth. 'He's not like a Muggot or a Huffaluk.'

'New monsters always look a bit weird at first,' she whispered. 'You soon get used to them though,' she said, stepping back with a start as the sheet of glass suddenly slid to one side like a door on the *Starship Enterprise.*

'Nelly!' gushed the broad gaping mouth. 'How wonderful to meet you!'

Nelly's dad gulped big time as the long, thin, newt-like fingers, entwined themselves around his wrist.

'Actually, I'm Nelly,' said Nelly. 'That's my dad!' she giggled, holding out her hand for an introduction.

'Oops!' said the Ultravore, releasing Nelly's dad and then weedling its sinuous fingers delicately around Nelly's outstretched wrist. 'Silly me!'

Nelly smiled and then shivered slightly.

Her wrist felt like it had been lassoed by wet shoelaces.

'Nelly, it is such a delight to meet you. My name is Pellion. Please do come inside, both of you.'

Nelly's dad wrung his wrist with the palm of his hand and then raised his hand politely.

'Actually, that's very kind of you, Pellion, but I am just the taxi driver. Nelly is the monster sitter; dropping off and picking up is my job!' He smiled.

A frogspawn-type cluster of sapphire-blue eyes blinked back warmly from the crown of Pellion's head.

'Of course of course, it's been very nice to meet you Mr Monster Sitter's Dad . . .'

'Clifford,' coughed Nelly's dad, 'call me Clifford.'

Nelly smiled as the two fathers took a moment to acquaint themselves, and then seized the opportunity to study the features of the monster standing before her.

Apart from his obvious friendliness, there were

two things about Pellion that struck her most: the size of his head, and the patterning on his body.

The giant purple-lipped smile that stretched across his white frog-shaped face was a metre wide at least from dimple to dimple. His complexion was bobbly like a toad's, his nostrils were set high in his forehead and, although far from classically handsome, there was a refined, almost trendy look to the rest of him.

For just below his chin, a fold of black skin tumbled like a polo neck towards a slim amphibious body that was chequered with black and white geometric squares.

His legs were supermodel thin, white as snow and stiff as barbecue skewers.

'No knees!' thought Nelly. 'Ultravores have no knees!'

There were feet all right, just the two; newt-like in appearance, with four delicate sucker-tipped toes.

Oh and there was one other thing.

Just the one.

An arm.

One arm only. Slender and sleeved with black bobbly skin from shoulder to wrist, it had a black and white chequered hand that put Nelly in mind of a driving glove.

Two of the three slender chequered fingers entwined politely around Nelly's dad's wrist again, as the two fathers drew their conversation to a close.

'It's a pleasure to meet you, Clifford,' said Pellion. 'Sorry about the little misunderstanding.

'Well, I've certainly never been mistaken for my own daughter before!' laughed Nelly's dad.

'It won't happen again!' smiled Pellion, releasing Nelly's dad's wrist and then taking a step back into the hallway of his home.

'Why don't you two say your goodbyes,' said Pellion, 'and then, Nelly, when you're ready, come on in and say hello to my wife and two children. They are so looking forward to meeting you.'

Nelly nodded and then turned to her dad with a smile. 'Time to go,' she mouthed.

'Lovely to meet you, Pellion,' waved her dad. 'Have a great time out with your wife this evening. Are you going somewhere nice?'

'We'll be going somewhere beautiful!' grinned Pellion. 'Thanks to Nelly.'

Nelly kissed her dad, waved him back to the car, took a deep breath and then stepped excitedly through the entrance of the Utravores' home.

6

The instant Nelly entered the hallway of Unit 11, the front door closed behind her with a futuristic swoosh.

She turned and marvelled, as the transparency of the glass door magically vanished before her eyes, restoring complete blackout privacy to the home.

Nelly's pulse began to quicken. This was no ordinary industrial unit at all. And it was certainly no ordinary home either. Even by monster standards.

She turned away from the front door, pointed herself towards the archway that led to the lounge and reeled. The walls and floor of the Ultravores' hallway were paved with hexagonal mirror-glass tiles. Each tiny tile was only postage stamp in size, but collectively they created a honeycomb of reflections that was eye-boggling.

Nelly didn't know where to blink first, she'd never seen so many six-sided images of herself.

'Do you like the effect?' asked Pellion, poking his head through the archway and adding his purple-lipped smile to the reflections. 'It's the very latest in prismatic tiling.'

Nelly focused and then refocused.

'It's very modern!' she smiled. 'Ultra modern!' she added.

'Come and meet the wife and kids!' smiled Pellion, hooking a black and white chequered finger into the hallway, and coaxing Nelly towards the lounge.

Nelly looked down at her trainers and watched as a kaleidoscope of reflections bombarded off the mirrored floor from her soles.

'NELLLLYYYY!!!!' chorused three broad gaping mouths, as she stepped through the archway and entered the lounge. 'Hello, Nelly the monster sitter!' they gushed.

It was an ultra-friendly welcome, in fact the heads of the four Ultravores waiting to greet her had a combined smile approaching three metres long! The children's smiles were so wide they looked to Nelly like they were sucking coat hangers.

Pellion stood proudly alongside his family in the middle of the room as Nelly's eyes swung from each gaping mouth in turn.

Pellion's wife stepped forward with a stiff-legged curtsey and introduced herself.

'Hello, Nelly, it's an absolute pleasure to meet you. My name is Willinika,' she smiled, thrusting her lips just centimetres from her face and hair, drying Nelly's face with two steaming puffs of hot and acrid breath.

Nelly's nostrils twitched and her eyes began to water. Willinika's breath stank like a fisherman's maggot box.

'It's lovely to meet you too!' smiled Nelly, discreetly pushing Willinika away from her face by extending her arm for a handshake.

Willinika obliged, stepping back, and then looped two snail-horn fingers around Nelly's wrist. With a grin and a gentle tug, she led Nelly across the room to meet the children.

'This is Lorice and this is Yerk,' beamed Willinika, nodding to the two smaller Ultravores standing excitedly beside their father.

'Hello, Lorice and Yerk!' smiled Nelly, stepping forward for handshakes three and four.

The two children raised their arms in turn and then hopped from side to side on legs as stiff as stilts.

'PapaPellion said he mistook your PapaClifford for you!' snorted the smaller of the two children. 'We think that's very funny, Nelly!'

Nelly smiled back into the little Ultravore's sparkling cluster of eyeballs and then laughed.

'Guess who's Lorice and guess who's Yerk!' said the other child, moving around the room with stiff-legged hops.

'Er . . .' said Nelly, not really knowing where to start. 'You might need to give me some clues!'

'Lorice is our daughter and Yerk is our son,' smiled Pellion less than helpfully.

Nelly's eyes widened, as her powers of deduction momentarily faltered.

She knew Pellion was a male Ultravore and that he had purple lips. The smaller of the two children had purple lips too. Perhaps that made it the son? Willinika had yellow lips and she was a female Ultravore. The taller of the two children had yellow lips too and so surely that made her the daughter?

Except . . . and this was a big except . . . the patterns on their bodies were different. The black and white chequered pattern that Pellion had on his body was shared not by the smaller child but the taller. And the black and white harlequin pattern that Willinika had on her body was shared not by the taller child, but the smaller.

Nelly's brow furrowed deeply as she determined which way to go.

Lips or patterns? Patterns or lips?

She decided to go patterns.

'I think . . .' she murmured, 'I think you are Lorice.' She smiled, pointing to the diamonds on the chest of the smaller child. 'And you are Yerk,' she laughed, prodding a chequered square on the chest of the taller child.

'Correct!' chuckled Yerk, taking his sister by the hand and skipping with her around the room.

'Good start!' thought Nelly. 'Good start!'

7

With four smiling Ultravores seated before her, Nelly took her first real chance to check out the ultra-modern decor of the lounge.

If 'ultra modern' had been Nelly's impression of the Ultravores' hallway then her verdict on the lounge was ultra off the scale.

The furnishings were kind of minimal. A sculpted stool for Nelly to sit on had been carried in from another room, and with the exception of a high-legged table tucked tightly against one wall there was no other furniture to see or mention.

Decor-wise, the hexagonal tiled theme of the hallway had been carried through to the lounge too. Far bigger than the mirror-glass tiles used in the hallway, each wall and floor tile honeycombed two metres across at its widest, and was fashioned from the most exquisitely polished white marble.

The black glass of the lounge's wide rectangular window cut a starkly contrasting swathe across the front of the room, giving the lounge a cool and contemporary feel. And yet, rather bizarrely, either side of the same window drab, brown, spiralling curtains were hanging.

'I wouldn't hang those in my home,' thought Nelly, staring across the room at the paper-thin curtains. 'They look like giant potato peelings!'

For sure the curtains were a curious addition to the Ultravores' lounge, but they were nothing compared to the lighting system that completely dominated the room at ceiling level.

'We'll feed the children before we go out,' said Willinika, slipping from her stool and then pointing casually up at the ceiling with a harlequin-patterned finger.

Nelly followed the direction of Willinika's finger and stared upwards at a never-ending spiral of fine glass tubing. Coiling like a snake from the centre of the ceiling to the very edges of the walls, the delicate white glass loops looked for all the world like a curly wurly wurly wurly wurly strip light. Stranger still, the lighting tube itself was sleeved by a fine coil of tightly sprung wire.

Unable to interpret the significance of what Willinika was saying, Nelly simply stared at the ceiling coils and nodded.

'Are you hungry, Nelly?' asked Lorice, hopping down from her stool. 'You can have some dinner with us if you like!'

Nelly lowered her eyes and smiled. 'That's very kind of you!' she laughed. 'And what might we be having?'

'Flies, of course!' cheered Yerk.

'Flies?' gasped Nelly. 'Did Yerk say FLIES?'

8

'Maybe he said fries, not flies,' thought Nelly, hovering in the lounge with the two children as Pellion and Willinika went to their bedroom to freshen up. 'French fries, hopefully.'

'We'll eat in the kitchen, children,' said Willinika, returning a couple of minutes later, sporting lips as black as coal.

Lorice and Yerk circled Nelly excitedly and then dragged her from the lounge in the direction of the kitchen.

'Don't be too rough,' smiled Pellion, 'or Nelly won't want to come to visit us again!'

Nelly padded cautiously across the white marble floor and then lurched through a second archway into a room much smaller than the lounge.

'This is our kitchen, Nelly!' smiled Willinika.

'It's a little on the small side but it does the job!'

Nelly blinked a honeycomb of blinks. The Ultravores' kitchen was a cross between Frankenstein's laboratory and a funfair hall of hexagonal mirrors.

Giant lighting coils sleeved with wire dominated the ceiling plus THREE of the walls, but, even weirder, a giant industrial-looking kitchen appliance towered from the centre of the floor.

'This is our Fli-Mincer,' grinned Willinika. 'Perhaps you have one at home?'

Nelly shook her head.

Monstrous in size, modern in design, it comprised a giant chromium funnel supported by three swimming-pool-flume-sized clear plastic tubes. Each of the see-through tubes dropped like pillars into large square chromium cabinet below, but what they did and how they worked was anybody's guess.

Nelly peered up at the giant funnel. It was almost as broad as the ceiling itself, and was centred perhaps a metre below the loop of the giant ceiling coil.

'Would you seal the doorway, please, dear,' said Willinika.

Pellion smiled and placed the palm of his chequered hand flat against the wall.

A black glass door slid from the wall, sealing the opening between the kitchen and the lounge.

'Kitchen sealed, love,' he smiled.

'Ready?' said Willinika, picking up a small remote control fob from the surface of the chromium cabinet.

'Ready!' beamed the children with licks of their lips.

Nelly double-took. Was that one tongue or three tongues?

'Ultra-light on,' said Willinika, pointing the fob at the ceiling.

Nelly threw puzzled looks at both children in turn and then slapped her hands across her eyes sharply as the kitchen suddenly exploded with green ultraviolet light.

'Window opening!' smiled Pellion.

Nelly scissored open two of her fingers and peeped out. The kitchen was bathed in green light. She squinted through her fingers again. The giant ultraviolet coils on the ceiling and walls had begun to hum, and the sleeves of coiled wire had started to glow.

Willinika lowered the fob from the ceiling and redirected it towards the kitchen window.

With a single stab of the fob, the impenetrable black glass of the rectangular window pane turned clear immediately and then instantly began to spatter with a barrage of guts and goo.

'Flies!' gasped Nelly. 'Flies are hurling themselves at the kitchen window!'

'It's the ultraviolet light!' beamed Pellion. 'We can attract flies from miles around with our ultraviolet lighting system! The mirror tiles magnify the frequency a millionfold and more!'

Nelly shuddered and then dropped to the floor with her head in her hands. The kitchen window had slid open!

'Tuck in, kids!' laughed Willinika, vanishing from view as the kitchen became engulfed in a choking cloud of suicidal flies.

Nelly covered her head with her arms, shut her eyes and zipped her lips tight shut. All around her, wings were singeing and fly carcasses were smoking.

'They're insect-ocutors not light coils!' she gasped. 'That's what the wire sleeving is for.' She shuddered. 'For electrocuting flies!'

She was both right and wrong, for the Ultravores' ultraviolet lighting system had a dual purpose: to attract flies first and zap them second.

Nelly opened one eye gingerly. The black glass of the kitchen window was closing again and the plague of flies was thinning.

All around her, flies were dropping like . . . well, flies. Those that dropped to the floor were being shovelled into the chromium funnel by Pellion and Willinika.

The rest were being plucked from the air as they tumbled, by the whip-cracking tongues of the two children.

'YUM YUM!' gulped Lorice, snapping up three flies in free fall at the same time.

'Three tongues!' gulped Nelly. 'I was right! They HAVE got three tongues at least!'

'DELISH!' grinned Yerk, clamping his jaws down on a second spadeful.

'Why don't you try some, Nelly!' munched Lorice. 'You'll love them!'

Nelly smiled weakly at each Ultravore in turn. 'Er, no thanks, flies aren't really my thing. I'm more of a fish finger person myself.'

'URRRGGHHHH!' shuddered Lorice with her mouthful. 'Did you hear that! Nelly likes eating fingers of fish!'

'How disgusting!' giggled Yerk with a crunch.

'Now now, children,' smiled Pellion, 'don't forget Nelly is a guest in our home. If Nelly wants to bite the fingers off fish, then that's entirely up to her. Each to their own, I say.'

'Hear hear,' agreed Willinika, raising another shovel of zapped flies and tipping them into Yerk's eager gaping mouth.

'No wonder their breath smells like a fisherman's bait box,' Nelly thought with a shudder. 'Flies are precisely what maggots turn into!'

In true monster sitting style Nelly politely watched as the children finished their dinners.

With Pellion and Willinika satisfied that their children's bellies were well and truly full, the remaining pile of flies were swept up and shovelled into the funnel.

'We'll mince those later,' said Willinika, running her hand lightly across the three clear plastic tubes. 'We have enough flies here to make pâté for a week!'

'Perhaps you could sort them with Nelly, children, after we've gone!' smiled Pellion. 'It will give you all something to do while we're away.'

Nelly peered grimly at the Fli-Mincer. If sorting flies even remotely involved eating flies or even tasting flies, then she was going to need an escape plan fast.

Lorice burped loudly and then rubbed her hand across her harlequin-patterned tummy.

'Will do,' she smiled. 'I'M FULLLLLL!'

'ME TOO!' belched Yerk.

'Then we'll be off, children!' smiled Pellion. 'Your mama and I have the sewage plant to visit!'

'THE SEWAGE PLANT!' blurted Nelly.

'Oh yes!' grinned Willinika, pointing the

remote control at the ceiling and deactivating the ultraviolet coils. 'Imagine the flies that we'll see there!'

9

Ultra friendly. Ultra modern. Ultraviolet.

A theme was developing here.

As Nelly waved goodbye to Pellion and Willinika she felt ultra certain that their home had more shocks and surprises in store.

'See you at eight!' she waved as they turned the corner of Unit 3 and vanished from view.

It was nearly six o'clock. By Nelly's reckoning, even with the briskest of stiff-legged walks, it would be a good half an hour at least before they arrived at the sewage works.

'Sewage works indeed!' she smiled, as the glass front door slid shut behind her. 'Of all the places to go and visit, they choose a stinky sewage plant!'

'Come on, Nelly,' grinned Lorice, hooking her finger around the archway like her papa had earlier, and drawing Nelly back to the lounge.

'Come and help us sort the flies!'

Nelly half smiled back at her from the end of the hall and then peered up at the ceiling and frowned.

'Why are there no ultraviolet coils in the hallway?' she asked the children as she entered the lounge. 'The walls and floor are tiled the same way as the kitchen but there are no coils on the ceiling or the walls.'

'Papa ordered too many tiles for the kitchen, that's all,' explained Yerk. 'So he used the ones that were left over to decorate the hall.'

'Oh,' said Nelly, expecting a far more irrational answer than that.

'We only need ultraviolet lighting in the kitchen and the lounge,' explained Yerk. 'The big tubes in the kitchen are the ones we use all the time, the smaller ones in the lounge are just a back-up.'

'In case of emergencies,' added Lorice.

Nelly nodded uncertainly. 'What kind of emergencies?' she asked.

'Like when there aren't many flies around,' replied Yerk.

'Like in the winter,' expanded Lorice. 'In the winter we might need to boost the ultraviolet lighting to make sure we catch enough flies.'

'We do that by lighting up both rooms,' said Lorice.

'And opening both windows,' smiled Yerk.

'The security guard said he'd seen some bright lights coming from here,' said Nelly.

'That would be us fly-zapping!' giggled Lorice.

Nelly perched herself on a stool for a moment and worked the Ultravores' fly-zapping system through her mind.

Step one. Seal the room.
Step two. Turn the ultraviolet coils on.
Step three. Turn the black window transparent.
Step four. Open the window.
Step five. Bring on the flies.
Step six. Close the window, and turn the transparent glass back to black.
Step seven. Trap and zap the flies.
Step eight. Turn off the ultraviolet coils.

Step nine. Unseal the room.
Step ten. Eat, shovel or mince.

It was ultra disgusting. But undeniably ingenious.

'Why are the wall tiles different in here?' asked Nelly, pointing to the giant honeycomb of hexagonal tiles that stretched across the white marble walls of the lounge.

'It confuses the flies,' grinned Lorice. 'Did you know that when flies look at things, they see them in the shape of hexagons, lots of tiny hexagons?'

Nelly shook her head. No, she didn't know that.

'It's called fly vision,' said Yerk.

Nelly nodded her head. Yes, she kind of did know that.

'When flies fly into our kitchen, our tiny hexagonal mirror tiles send their fly vision doolally,' chuckled Lorice.

'And if we let them into our lounge without being zapped, the big white hexagonal tiles in there make them doubly confused.'

'Confused flies are far more easy to catch with your tongues,' grinned Yerk.

'And eat!' slurped Lorice.

Nelly puffed out her cheeks. She had no idea the science of catching flies could be so complicated. All her mum and dad ever used was a rolled-up newspaper.

'If you don't mind me asking,' she murmured, 'exactly how many tongues do you have?'

'Three each!' laughed Yerk. 'A blue one for bluebottles, a green one for greenbottles and a yellow one for wasps!'

'You eat wasps as well!' gasped Nelly.

'If they're in season, yes!' laughed Lorice.

Nelly shook her head in wonderment. 'Don't the wasps sting your tongue when you catch them?' she asked.

'Not if we use our yellow tongue,' said Lorice, unfurling an egg-yolk-coloured tongue like a trouser belt and letting it drop from her chin to the floor.

'If we use these it would sting,' grinned Yerk, flicking a navy-blue tongue sideways from one corner of his mouth and then darting a green tongue out from the other.

'Blimey,' thought Nelly. 'And I thought I'd seen it all!'

'Let's go and sort the flies, Nelly!' grinned Lorice. 'Mama and Papa will be really pleased if we sort the flies before they get home! You can help us make the pâté!

'We make three types,' explained Lorice. 'Green pâté, blue pâté and mixed!'

Nelly allowed them to lead her back through

the archway into the kitchen, but deliberately slowed each step she took to allow herself time to think of an evasive plan.

'If they try and make me taste their pâtés, I'll have a coughing fit,' she thought. 'If they try and get me to swallow a shovelful, I'll just pretend to faint.'

'This is how we sort the flies,' Lorice reached under the polished steel lip of the chromium cabinet and fumbled for a switch.

'We just flick this switch here and . . .'

Nelly shielded her eyes with her hand and clamped her lips tight shut, as the huge chromium funnel at the top of the contraption began to vibrate.

'Da daaahhh!' chuckled Yerk.

With the flick of a second switch each of the flume-sized tubes instantly filled with liquidized mush. Fly guts, fly wings, fly legs and fly brains spattered and spun before Nelly's horrified eyes into something approaching whipped cream.

'The green paste is made from greenbottle flies,' grinned Lorice, pointing to the column on

Nelly's left. 'The blue paste is made from bluebottle flies . . .' she said, pointing to the column on Nelly's right.

'And the paste in the middle is a blend!' beamed Yerk. 'You know, a mixture of any other type of fly we might have caught. The Fli-Mincer sorts all the flies out into the right tubes.'

'Like Asti's coin sorter!' thought Nelly.

'It doesn't mince butterflies too, does it?' she grimaced.

'Sometimes, yes!' Lorice told her with a triple lick of her lips.

'Dragonflies?' ventured Nelly.

'In the summertime, yes,' smiled Yerk. 'Dragonflies make the paste quite crunchy.'

'Sorted!' Yerk exclaimed, tapping the giant funnel with his hand to dislodge any fly that might not have tumbled its way into the correct tube.

Lorice brought the funnel vibrations to a halt with a flick of the switch. Nelly stepped forward and braved a closer look.

'I'm going to be sick,' she thought as three types of freshly whipped fly paste slid unappetizingly past her eyes down their respective tubes.

Gloop by gloop, dollop by dollop, they oozed into the steel storage unit below.

'Would you like to try some, Nelly?' slurped Lorice.

'No, thank you,' said Nelly, hoping that a polite refusal would be the end of the matter.

She was in luck. There was no need for a coughing fit or a fainting show; both Ultravore children seemed happy to return to the lounge.

'Do the fly sorter tubes need washing up?' asked Nelly, praying the answer would be no.

'Yes, they do,' said Lorice with a shrug. 'But Mama and Papa will do that when they get home.'

'Phew!' thought Nelly, striding through the kitchen archway and escaping back to the lounge.

10

'You're home is ultra trendy, isn't it,' said Nelly, easing her bottom back on to her stool.

'What does trendy mean?' asked Lorice, pulling her own stool alongside Nelly's.

'Modern,' said Nelly. 'Your house is full of ultra-modern things.'

'That's because we're Ultravores, I suppose!' laughed Yerk, completing the triangle with his own stool.

'Don't you have trendy things in your home, Nelly?' asked Lorice.

Nelly thought for a moment. Their TV wasn't a plasma, their music system was ten years old, her dad's record collection belonged in a museum. Their lighting system used nothing more than ordinary light bulbs, the glass in their windows didn't change colour, and all the doors had handles instead of fingerprint activation.

'About the trendiest thing in our house is my electric toothbrush,' sighed Nelly.

'What's an electric toothbrush?' asked Yerk.

'It's a brush for cleaning your teeth,' said Nelly. 'It runs on batteries so you don't have to move the bristles up and down with your hand.'

'Why do you clean your teeth?' asked Lorice, craning her wide, frog-like face forward to catch a glimpse of the results.

'To keep them white,' said Nelly, obliging with a big toothy grin.

'But our teeth are orange,' replied Lorice, a little puzzled. 'I wouldn't want mine to be white, they'd look funny.'

'Er . . . everyone has white teeth where I live,' Nelly said. 'All my friends do too.'

'We don't,' grinned Yerk.

'That would account for the stink of maggots,' thought Nelly.

Nelly shrugged her shoulders and placed her palms on her knees.

'My sister Asti thinks she is the trendiest thing in our house, but she's just a fashion victim.'

'How old is your sister?' asked Lorice.

'Five minutes older than me!' smiled Nelly. 'We're twins.'

'So your mama laid two eggs at once!' gasped Lorice.

'Er no, humans don't lay eggs,' said Nelly.

'What do you lay then?' asked Yerk, keen to learn more.

Nelly puffed out her cheeks. 'Er, we don't lay anything,' she blustered. 'We . . . er . . . well, we just don't lay eggs.'

'What do you do then?' asked Lorice, pulling her stool a little closer.

Nelly's cheeks flushed red. She really didn't want to be getting into a conversation about human reproduction.

'My sister wants to have her belly button pierced,' said Nelly, deliberately changing the subject. 'There's a disco after school on Monday, and she wants to wear a belly-button stud so that she can impress Darren Leadbetter. She thinks it will make him like her, but my mum and dad won't let her.'

'What's a belly button?' asked Yerk.

Nelly lifted up her sardine T-shirt and presented hers to the two children.

'We haven't got one of those,' said Lorice.

'All humans have them,' said Nelly, pulling her shirt back down. 'We have them from birth.'

'Why haven't we got belly buttons?' asked Yerk, staring blankly down at his midriff.

'Probably because you hatched from an egg, whereas I came out of . . .' Nelly faltered. The conversation was going full circle and was in danger of pointing back to the birds and bees.

'Your lights are much cooler than ours,' she said, changing the subject rather blatantly this time.

'You can turn them on if you like,' said Yerk, giving up on the prospect of a belly button and staring up at the ceiling. 'There are no mirror tiles in here so they won't be as bright.'

Nelly looked at the white marble walls, and then turned anxiously towards the lounge window.

'If I turn the lights on, the room won't fill up

with flies, will it?' she asked.

'No!' laughed Lorice, 'the window is closed and the glass is black, the flies won't be able to see you or the lights!'

A smile crept across Nelly's face. 'I do think the ultraviolet green looks kind of cool,' she grinned. 'We only have white bulbs at home.'

'I'll go and get the fob from the kitchen,' grinned Yerk.

Nelly placed her hands under her bottom and peered enviously around the room. The ultra-modern lighting, the doors, the glass, the tiles, made 117 Sweet Street seem positively Victorian.

'Here you are, Nelly,' smiled Yerk, returning with the fob. 'The top button controls the lights, the bottom button controls the windows.'

Nelly pulled her hands from under her bottom, plucked the fob from Yerk's fingers and cautiously held it up before her eyes.

'Say that again,' she murmured nervously. 'I don't want to start activating windows by mistake!'

'Let me show you, Nelly,' laughed Lorice. She slipped from her stool and wrapped her slender harlequin-patterned arm around Nelly's shoulder.

'This button here does the windows,' she whispered, drawing the corner of her smiling mouth close up to Nelly's. 'And this one does the lights.'

Nelly watched the tip of Lorice's finger flick from the bottom of the fob to the top, and then grimaced as a puff of fly muncher's breath assaulted her nostrils.

'I've got it!' she gasped, pulling away from the stench as politely as she possibly could. 'Top for lights, bottom for windows.'

'She's got it,' said Yerk, grinning at his sister.

'Here goes!' said Nelly. She pointed the fob up at the ceiling and pressed the top button with her thumb.

There was a flicker, followed by a hum, before the entire room detonated into a riot of green ultraviolet light.

'It's amazing!' Nelly squinted, her eyes blinking to adjust to the change. 'Look, the two of you have turned black and green!'

'You look green too, Nelly,' laughed Yerk,

pointing to Nelly's face.

'I thought ultraviolet light was purple or blue,' Nelly marvelled.

'It can be,' smiled Lorice, 'but the best colour to attract flies and insects is green.'

'Well, you learn something every day!' laughed Nelly. 'Can we keep the lights on?' she begged. 'It's ultra fun with the lights on.'

The Ultravores smiled at each other with a shrug. When it came to things ultraviolet they had seen it all before, but if it kept Nelly entertained, they were happy to oblige.

'Now what shall we do?' asked Yerk.

'Something green and ghostly!' smiled Nelly.

11

'What's a ghostly?' asked Yerk.

'You mean a ghost,' said Nelly. 'What's a ghost.'

'Do I?' asked Yerk.

'Yes, you do,' explained Nelly. 'It's not a ghost*ly*, it's a ghost. A ghost is a dead person that comes back to life to haunt you. Ghosts are ghost*ly*, ghostlies can't be ghosts, if you see what I mean,' said Nelly, slightly confusing herself.

Yerk looked at his sister with a cluster of puzzled eyes.

'Sometimes ghosts keep their heads under their arms and rattle chains at you when you're asleep!' cackled Nelly, trying her best to milk the zombie-green atmosphere for all it was worth.

'How can a ghost be alive if it's dead?' asked Lorice, more than a little unconvinced.

'Ghosts aren't alive,' said Nelly. 'They were

alive, until they died, but then they come alive again, and walk around as though they are alive even though they are dead . . . think,' said Nelly with a scratch of her head. This was more complicated than explaining the rules of cricket!

'So they're dead, but they can walk around?' asked Lorice.

'Yes,' said Nelly. 'Because they are the walking dead.'

'So they're not alive?' asked Yerk.

'No,' said Nelly.

'They're dead?' asked Lorice.

'But they can still walk?' asked Yerk.

'With their head off?' asked Lorice.

Nelly sighed, and placed the heels of her trainers on the rungs of her stool.

'Actually,' she groaned, 'let's not do something green and ghostly, let's do something green and not ghostly at all.'

'Like what?' grinned Lorice.

'Liiiiike . . .' Nelly peered around the lounge for inspiration. 'Liiiiiiiiiiiiiiiiiiiike . . . murder in the dark!'

'It's not dark,' said Lorice.

Nelly nibbled her lip. 'All right, murder in the green!' she said with a flash of inspiration.

'How do you play that?' asked Yerk, more than a little intrigued.

'I'll show you,' said Nelly. 'Cover your eyes and count to a hundred while I hide somewhere in the house. When you've counted to a hundred you can come and look for me, and when you find me, you have to pretend to murder me.'

'Not murder you for real?' asked Lorice.

'No, Lorice,' sighed Nelly. 'If you murder me for real, I won't be able to monster sit for you, will I? Plus you won't be able to have your turn to hide, because I'll be too dead to look for you.'

'Unless you're a ghost,' said Yerk.

'Just checking you didn't want to be murdered,' said Lorice with a grin.

'No, I don't,' sighed Nelly.

'Good job I asked!'

'OK then,' said Nelly, positioning both of

the Ultravore children on their stools. 'Cover your eyes.'

'My hand is too small to cover all of my eyes at once,' said Lorice.

'Mine too,' said Yerk.

Nelly peered at the cluster of eyeballs wobbling like frogspawn on the crowns of the two children's heads. They had a point.

'OK, turn round and face the other way then,' said Nelly, 'and NO PEEKING!'

Lorice and Yerk did as they were told, swivelled round on their stools to face the kitchen and began their count from one to a hundred.

The moment their backs were turned, Nelly made a dash for the curtains.

'. . . ninety-seven, ninety-eight, ninety-nine, one hundred!'

'We're coming, Nelly!' chuckled Yerk.

'To murder you!' giggled Lorice.

'Not really!' grinned Yerk. 'Only pretend murder you!'

The two Ultravore children wheeled round on their stools and laughed out loud.

'Seen you!' chuckled Lorice, raising her arm immediately and pointing to where Nelly could clearly be seen kicking and thrashing beside the window.

'Seen you too!' laughed Yerk, following the line of his sister's outstretched finger.

'HELLLLLLLLLPPPP!' squealed Nelly in a blind panic.

'I'm stuck to the curtains!'

12

Lorice and Yerk slipped from their stools and scampered across the lounge towards the window.

'Get them off me!' Nelly thrashed, flapping her arms and legs like a fly trapped in a spider's web. 'Your curtains are sticky!' she gasped. 'Why didn't you tell me that your curtains were sticky!'

'You didn't ask,' shrugged Lorice.

Nelly was in a big trouble. The large paper-thin coils of the drab brown curtains had wrapped themselves around her body like a gluey cocoon.

Each time she thrashed out with her elbows to break free, more of the gluey pleats held her fast. Each time she kicked out with her feet, another fold in the curtains clamped to another part of her leg.

Nelly gritted her teeth and then stamped her right foot down hard. The lace of her trainer unfurled like ribbon pasta and then stuck to another spiral of the curtains.

'Anyway,' said Yerk. 'They're not curtains . . .'

'They're flypapers,' explained Lorice.

'FLYPAPERS!' gasped Nelly, thrashing and twisting and wrenching for all she was worth.

'I'm not a fly I'm a babysitter!'

'We're not babies,' said Yerk, a little offended.

'Monsters, I mean!' gasped Nelly.

Lorice and Yerk stood helplessly by and watched as Nelly's attempts to break free from the paper succeeded only in wrapping herself further up amongst the sticky paper folds.

'Get me out!' she panted after another fit of

yanks, thrashes and jerks. For the first time that evening the broad smiles of the Utravore children switched to deep furrowed frowns. After all, the primary function of the Ultavores' giant flypapers was to trap, and trap big time. To Nelly's misfortune, that's precisely what they had done.

Lorice and Yerks' clusters of frogspawn-jelly eyes stared anxiously in the direction of the window.

One side of Nelly's face, including the corner of her mouth, was stuck fast now, and her ponytail was glued in a looping arc above her head to another fold. One of her arms was pinned high above her head as though she was answering a question in class, her other arm was folded in an armlock behind her waist. One leg of her jeans looked as though it was about to score a goal, and the other was completely lost to view, wrapped like an Egyptian mummy in coil upon coil of sticky paper.

'Why did you touch them in the first place, Nelly?' asked Lorice. 'They're only meant for flies.'

'I was going to hide behind them!' squawked Nelly from the other corner of her mouth. 'Most of the monsters' houses I visit have curtains, not giant flypapers! Why didn't someone tell me they were sticky!'

Lorice and Yerk looked at each other. Neither had an answer.

'We never really take much notice of them to be honest,' said Yerk. 'They're only there for ultra emergencies. Like if there's a power cut and the ultraviolet lights won't switch on. Papa says if there's an ultra emergency like that we will need something else to catch our flies with.'

'Like big flypapers,' added Yerk.

'Well, you've got an ultra emergency now!' groaned Nelly as the eyelashes of her right eye clung to another fold in the curtains. 'I'm trapped here, and if you don't get me out I'll be stuck here for good!'

'What are we going to do?' asked Lorice.

'You'll have to pull me out!' said Nelly.

Yerk looked at his sister, and then stared down at the chequered fingers of his hand.

'But we've only got one arm each, Nelly, and we can only reach up to your waist.'

'Well, try anyway!' gasped Nelly, twisting the other way and then wishing she hadn't.

'But what if we get stuck to the curtains too?' asked Lorice rather sensibly.

Nelly sighed. Lorice was right. The chances of the two children being strong enough to wrench her free from the flypaper were slimmer than slim. Not only that, but as their monster sitter and guardian she had a duty to ensure that neither of the children came to any harm while their parents were away.

'I'm sure Mama and Papa will be able to pull you out,' said Lorice in a far from convincing whisper.

'I can't stay wrapped up in curtains until eight o'clock!' gasped Nelly. 'I'm meant to be looking after you! How can I look after you if my arms and legs are glued to the curtains?'

'They're not curtains, they're . . .'

'I know they're flypapers!' growled Nelly, starting to feel more than a little hot under the collar. 'But they looked like curtains to me!'

'I was just saying,' apologized Yerk.

'Well, don't SAY anything, DO something!' said Nelly with uncharacteristic tetchiness. 'DO SOMETHING FAST!'

Yerk and Lorice turned full circle one way, full circle the other and then faced each other with downturned mouths.

'We could shout for help!' suggested Lorice with a stiff-legged hop.

'Good idea!' said Nelly. 'Three voices at once, let's all shout for help!'

'But our windows are ultra-glazed,' said Yerk. 'No one will be able to hear us through ultra-glazing.'

'THEN OPEN THE WINDOW!' commanded Nelly. 'Open the window, and then after the count of three, shout at the top of your voices.'

Yerk ran back to the kitchen and grabbed the control fob from the counter.

'Window opening!' he puffed, racing back into the lounge and directing the fob at at the curtains.

The large black glass pane of the ultra-glazed lounge window slid open in an instant.

'ONE, TWO . . . NOOOOOOOOOOOO!!!!!!!!'
gasped Nelly, suddenly realizing the mistake she had made!

13

'SHUT THEM—' squealed Nelly, but it was too late.

In the beat of a wasp's wing, the Ultravores' lounge filled with a choking black cloud of manically buzzing flies.

Nelly thrashed and choked as the ultraviolet ceiling coil began to crackle and the lounge filled with smoky green air.

'OOPS!' said Lorice, tugging her brother's attention away from the ceiling light and pointing him in the direction of Nelly.

The sticky brown coils of flypaper were now thick with wriggling flies too!

Nelly zipped her lips tight. A minute ago she was wearing her sardine T-shirt, green jeans and red trainers. Now she was wearing flies. It was nightmare land.

She had flies stuck to her face and flies

wriggling on the nape of her neck. Just millimetres from her ear she could hear fly wings buzzing like a forest full of chainsaws.

'Are you going to say three?' asked Lorice innocently. 'Or do you want us to shout now?'

Nelly parted her lips to reply, and then shut them fast as a mouthful of airborne flies bounced off the enamel of her teeth.

'Shut the windowwww!' squeaked Nelly through gritted teeth.

'What did she say?' slurped Yerk, unable to resist snaffling a quick snack with his tongues.

'I think she said shut the window,' said Lorice, plucking a greenbottle from mid-air with her green tongue, and then dispatching it down her gullet with a soft crunch.

Yerk pointed the fob high up in the direction of the window and sealed the room with a click of the button.

'Turn the light off,' squeaked Nelly, her forehead teeming with flies.

Yerk jabbed the fob at the ceiling and then lowered his arm as the ultraviolet green vanished from the room.

To Nelly's immense relief the dense cloud of flies began to thin instantly.

She waited, suspended amongst the curtains, as the crackle of smoking fly wings finally faded away.

Satisfied the worst was over, Nelly determined to open her eyes.

She fluttered one eyelid open cautiously and surveyed the room.

Lorice and Yerk were standing before her, knee deep in a carpet of stunned flies.

Above them the ultraviolet ceiling coil was smoking like a gun barrel.

'ARE YOU SURE YOU'VE SHUT THE WINDOW!' garbled Nelly, unable to twist her body round far enough to check.

Lorice looked at Yerk and smiled broadly.

'It's all right, Nelly,' she grinned. 'You can open your mouth now!'

Yerk nodded. 'The window is closed, but actually it's the ultraviolet light that attracts the flies, not the open window. The flypaper only traps them if they just happen to fly in.'

Nelly groaned and then finally mustered the courage to part her teeth. The spattering of bluebottles plastered to the right side of her face wriggled frantically as she loosened her jaw.

'We need to think of another plan,' she whimpered.

Lorice bent down and scooped a palmful of assorted flies into her mouth. 'I'm not very good at thinking of plans,' she said with a munch.

'Me neither,' said Yerk, using his blue tongue to pluck twenty or thirty bluebottles from the carpet in quick succession.

'I know!' said Nelly, forcing a half-smile from the side of her face that wasn't stuck to the curtains. 'What IS the matter with me! I'll do what I always do when I get in a bit of a monster-sitting fix. I'll ring for monster help! Grit's my Huffaluk friend! He's got three arms! He'll be able to pull me out of these curtains for sure! All we need to do is ring him on my mobile phone!'

'Where's your mobile phone?' asked Lorice.

'It's in the back pocket of my jeans,' said Nelly

'Where's the back pocket of your jeans?' asked Yerk.

Nelly angled her head downwards as best she could and peered past the wriggling folds of fly-encrusted curtains.

One of her arms was still pinned above her head, the other still trapped behind her back, but there would have been little use in her pointing. Her mobile was completely and inaccessibly entombed in tightly spiralling bandages of ultra-sticky flypaper.

Ringing a Huffaluk, or anyone, for help was not an option.

'We're going to have to shout for help again,' she sighed.

'But no one will hear us with the window

closed,' frowned Lorice.

Nelly's shoulders sagged.

'OK, I guess you'd better open the window again,' she sighed. 'But whatever you do, DON'T TURN ON THE LIGHTS.'

'I won't,' smiled Yerk, raising the control fob and pointing it at the window.

'Make sure you DON'T,' said Nelly sternly.

As the window opened, a warm evening breeze entered the room, causing the legs of the flies stuck to Nelly's face to wriggle infuriatingly.

'This better work,' groaned Nelly, relieved at least that no new flies seemed to be entering the lounge.

'Remember, on the count of three,' said Nelly, trying her best to ignore the vibration of frenzied wings, 'remember, we must all shout for help, at the very TOPS of our voices.'

Lorice and Yerk nodded, and then took ultra-deep breaths in readiness.

'ONE,' said Nelly.

'TWO,' nodded Nelly.

'THREE!'

14

As tops of voices went, the scream for HELLL LLLPPPPPP!!!!! was a little disappointing.

It wasn't so much Nelly's voice that had failed to reach the heights; Nelly had mustered so many decibels that her tonsils had nearly joined the zapped flies on the carpet.

No, it was the Ultravores' voices that had rather underperformed. In fact Nelly wasn't even sure she had even heard them shout.

'I said shout at the top of your voices!' she said, with a frustrated flap of the curtains.

'We *did* shout at the top of our voices,' protested Lorice.

'Well, you're going to have to shout a lot louder than that if anyone is going to hear us!' said Nelly. 'Now let's do it again after three: ONE, TWO, THREE!'

'HEEEEELLLLLLLLLPPPPPPPPPPPPPP!!!!' went Nelly.

'   ,' went the Ultravores.

'You did it again!' said Nelly, with a sharp jerk of her head. A greenbottle was trying to crawl up her nose.

'I know we did,' said Lorice, plucking it from Nelly's top lip with her green tongue.

'You asked us to?' said Yerk, a little confused.

'I asked you to SHOUT!' said Nelly, blinking rapidly as the blur of a fly's wing began vibrating just millimetres from her right eye.

'We did shout,' said Lorice.

'No, you DIDN'T!' shouted Nelly. 'YOU OPENED YOUR MOUTHS but nothing came out! That's not shouting, in fact it's not even WHISPERING!'

'It sounded like shouting to me,' said Yerk, looking at his sister.

'We did shout, Nelly, I promise,' said Lorice. 'Are you sure your ears aren't clogged up with flies?'

'Maybe they've crawled into her brain,' whispered Lorice.

Nelly's blood began to boil. Not only was she glued to some fly-encrusted curtains, not only was she unable to move her arms or her legs. Not only was one side of her face stuck down like a postage stamp, not only were her nostrils an open gateway for any insect that happened to pass, she was now having her sanity questioned by two fly-munching monster children.

'No, I haven't got flies in my ears *or* my brain!' she snapped. 'I can hear perfectly, thank you! I can hear the annoying buzz of a million upside-down fly wings trying to take off around me, I can hear tiny fly legs bending and straining to pull themselves free from the curtains,' she exaggerated, 'and I can even hear one little fly shouting HELP HELP HELP, a lot louder than you did!'

Lorice looked at Yerk and smiled. Considering Nelly was in such a predicament, that was quite a funny joke.

'I promise you, Nelly, we did shout as loud as we can,' said Yerk.

'Well, you need to shout louder,' said Nelly, 'as

in loud enough for someone to hear!'

'Let's try again, Yerk,' said Lorice, determined to pull her weight. 'I'll count to three this time.'

Nelly nodded with half her sticky face and conjured a secret plan.

'One,' said Lorice

'Two,' said Lorice

'Three!' said Lorice, opening her cavernous jaws wide.

'   ,' screamed the two children, their faces straining crimson and their eyeballs trembling like jelly.

Nelly wriggled with exasperation. She had deliberately withheld her own voice this time, and, just as she had suspected, there wasn't a sound from the Ultravores to be heard. Sure their mouths had opened, sure their eyeballs had wobbled but, sure as sure is sure, nothing whatsoever had come out of their mouths. Unless you include two giant puffs of steaming bait-box breath.

Nelly threw accusing stares at the brother and sister in turn.

'YOU SEE!' she said, thrashing in vain once again, 'I caught you out! I didn't make a sound that time, and NEITHER DID EITHER OF YOU!'

'Yes we did,' said Lorice.

'NO, YOU DIDN'T!' said Nelly.

'I thought we did,' said Yerk.

'Well, you thought wrong!' said Nelly, wrenching her elbows left and right with frustration. 'Just my luck,' she thought, 'just when I need to be monster sitting two monsters who can shout, I end up with two monsters who can only talk. Can you believe it? They can talk and be heard, but they can't shout and be heard?' It didn't make any sense at all.

Nelly gave up and let her body go limp.

It was hopeless. She could scream all she liked, she could wriggle all she liked, but she would be stuck like glue to the curtains until Pellion and Willinika returned home.

'You may as well close the window,' she sighed.

'Do you want me to turn the magni-light back on?' asked Yerk, pointing the control fob at the ceiling. 'The flies won't come in, and you really did like the green lighting!'

'If you like,' sighed Nelly. 'I'm past caring.'

15

'Sorry I can't help you tidy,' said Nelly, as Lorice lifted another shovel of flies from the carpet and carried it through to the kitchen.

Lorice looked up and grinned.

'You do look funny, Nelly,' she giggled. 'You look all jiggledy-joggledy with your arms and legs caught up like that.'

Nelly peered back with a half-smile. 'I suppose I probably do,' she sighed.

'Are you sure you don't want to taste some of these flies?' asked Yerk, sliding the blade of his shovel into a heap of zapped legs, bodies and wings. 'I'll pick the wasps out for you if you want.'

With her cheek stuck fast to the curtain, a half-shake of her head was all that Nelly could manage. However, she repeated the action vigorously, just in case Yerk thought she might have been tempted.

'Have you never eaten flies before, Nelly?' asked Lorice, returning from the kitchen. 'You're really missing out if you haven't.'

'I nearly ate a greenfly once,' said Nelly. 'It was on a lettuce leaf my mum had put in my salad.'

'Mmm, greenflies sound nice,' said Lorice, resting her chin for a moment on the handle of the shovel. 'Are they like greenbottle flies?'

'Smaller,' said Nelly. 'Much much smaller. I imagine if you zapped a greenfly there wouldn't be very much left of it to eat.'

'They still sound delicious,' said Lorice with a whip crack of her green tongue.

'I'll stick to lettuce,' smiled Nelly.

Shovel full by shovelful, the carpet of dead flies was removed from the floor of the Ultravores' lounge.

'Does anyone know what the time is?' called Nelly, as both children carried their shovels through the archway into the lounge.

'It's a quarter past . . .' shouted Yerk, switching on the Fli-Mincer, and drowning out the number seven.

Nelly dangled helplessly amongst the sticky coils of the curtains, and did some sums in her head. If it was a quarter past seven, and Pellion and Willinika were due back at eight o'clock then she had forty-five minutes of sticky torture still to endure.

'Your mum and dad will be back in three-quarters of an hour!' she shouted, doubtful that the children could hear her above the sound of the freshly zapped flies that were mincing through the tubes of the Fli-Mincer.

Nelly took a deep breath and prepared to holler again.

'I SAID YOUR MUM AND DAD WILL BE—'

Nelly stopped in mid-sentence and swivelled her free eye in the direction of the hallway arch.

To her complete surprise and huge relief, Pellion and Willinika had just burst into the room!

16

'Oh my goodness!' gasped Willinika, striding stiff-leggedly across to the curtains and staring jiggle-eyed at Nelly.

'What's happened to you!' gasped Pellion. 'And where are the children?'

Nelly dangled shamefaced from the curtains and tried in vain once again to prise her cheek from the flypaper coils.

'Er, I had a bit of an accident,' she said through the corner of her mouth. 'The children are fine, they're in the kitchen making pâté.'

Pellion and Willinika turned their broad gaping mouths in the direction of the kitchen archway and then turned back towards the tangle of flypaper spirals.

'You poor thing!' said Willinika, reaching forward to stroke Nelly's arm. 'We must get you out immediately.'

Pellion nodded in agreement, and then raised his chequered fingers to stroke his chin thoughtfully.

'I still don't understand what happened to you, Nelly,' he said, tugging at the sleeve of her T-shirt with a frown. 'The flypapers are meant to catch flies, not monster sitters.'

'Let's just say it was a game that went wrong,' sighed Nelly.

She dangled forlornly from the curtains as Willinika rushed into the kitchen to check on the kids and Pellion raced away in search of his tool kit.

He returned moments later carrying nothing more than a keyring-sized torch. Or so it appeared.

'Keep very still, Nelly,' he said, 'or it won't be just the flypaper I'll be cutting to shreds!'

Nelly's body stiffened as the chromium tube in Pellion's hand sprung to life like a miniature Jedi light sabre.

'It's a laser!' thought Nelly. 'Pellion's going to

do laser surgery on the curtains!'

Incision by incision, tangle by tangle, the Ultravore father set about freeing Nelly from her sticky tomb.

Nelly's nostrils twitched as the fine red beam of the laser sliced and sizzled its way through the spirals.

'This is making me quite hungry!' smiled Pellion. 'It smells just like Thursday lunch! Does your family have a roast on Thursdays, Nelly?'

'Sundays,' gasped Nelly, lowering her left arm the first time in over an hour. 'Not flies, though,' she added hastily.

'Soon have you out of here,' smiled Pellion, as another slice of the laser detached the curtains from her left leg.

Nelly looked over Pellion's shoulder as the broad smiling mouths of Willinika and the children returned to the lounge.

'Nearly free, Nelly?' chuckled Lorice.

'Nearly!' smiled Nelly.

'We're not allowed to use that,' said Yerk, pointing at the smoking beam of the laser.

'I'm not surprised!' said Nelly, pulling her right arm gingerly from behind her back and then staring ruefully at the large spiral of flypaper that was still glued to her sleeve.

'How am I going to get the sticky stuff off my clothes?' she murmured to herself.

'A strong soapy solution should do it,' mumbled Pellion, concentrating hard on a rather delicate piece of laser surgery that involved a diagonal slice alongside her hip, followed by a zig-zagging crimp-cut through three spirals, plus an incision along the angle of her left elbow.

Nelly held her breath as another slice of the laser sent the reek of smoking fly carcass wisping past her face.

'Just your cheek to go now, Nelly,' chuckled Pellion, with a puff of his black and white chequered chest. 'Then you'll be free!'

Nelly raised her thumbs and winked optimistically at the children. 'Keep very still, Nelly,' smiled Lorice, 'or Papa might cut your head off!'

'Real murder in the green!' giggled Yerk.

Nelly closed her eyes, and then stiffened extra stiffly as Pellion drew the laser beam upwards.

There was no need for her to worry. Rather than take any risks with Nelly's facial features Pellion kept a wide berth with the laser beam, slicing through the sticky paper coil a good distance from her cheek.

With a weary whoop of delight and relief, Nelly broke free from the curtains and wrapped her arms around Pellion's shoulders.

'Thank you!' she gasped, planting a big kiss somehere near the middle of Pellion's purple lips. 'Thank you so much for cutting me free!'

Willinika and the children laughed and clapped as Nelly kissed each of them in turn.

'It's so good to be able to move!' gasped Nelly, waving her arms and legs up and down like a demented puppet, 'I can't tell you how nice it is to be able to jump up and down, and move my head!'

'We're sorry your visit ended up like this,' smiled Willinika. 'It's our fault. We really should have warned you about the flypapers.'

'I thought I was going to be stuck in them until eight o'clock!' laughed Nelly, wrapping her arms around the childrens' shoulders. 'Why did you come home so early? Didn't you see any flies at the sewage works?'

'We heard the children's screams for help, Nelly,' said Pellion. 'There were some wonderful flies at the sewage works, but the instant we heard the children's screams we ran straight home!'

Nelly's jaw dropped open in disbelief.

'TOLD YOU!' laughed Lorice. 'I told you we were shouting at the top of our voices!'

Nelly looked at the two children, and then stared blankly at Willinika and Pellion in turn.

'But I never heard a thing when you were shouting!' she protested.

'Different frequency,' smiled Willinika. 'Ultravores have ultrasonic screams.'

'A human would never hear our screams; the sound frequencies we use are far too high.'

'Like a dog whistle?' Nelly asked.

'And higher!' smiled Willinika.

Nelly sighed one of the biggest sighs of her monster sitting career. To be honest, she hadn't ended up looking after two Ultravore children, two Ultravore children had ended up looking after her.

Not only had her visit been ultra modern, not only had it been ultraviolet, but ultra sticky, and now ultrasonic too!

How ultra cool was that?

And yet it was when her dad arrived to pick her up at eight o'clock that the biggest surprise of all was sprung.

'Have you seen all the animals that are sitting outside your front door?' gasped Nelly's dad, as he hurried with Pellion into the lounge.

'There's a PARROT, there's a DOG, there's a CAT, there's a TERRAPIN, THREE RABBITS and you're never going to believe this . . . there's even a SEA LION!'

Nelly rushed down the hall of the Ultravores' home and stared open-mouthed at the menagerie of animals that had gathered outside the doorway to Unit 11.

'That must be Fevvers!' she said, pointing to an African grey parrot hat was perched on the head of a chocolate Labrador. 'And these must be Benson and Shelley! But what are they doing here?' she gasped.

Lorice and Yerk tugged on her sleeve and pointed at their wide-open mouths.

'Your ultrasonic screams!' gasped Nelly. 'They were attracted by your ultrasonic screams!'

'Like a dog whistle!' smiled Pellion.

'And a terrapin whistle!' giggled Lorice.

'AND A SEA LION WHISTLE!' clapped Nelly.

'We came running when we heard the children screaming, and so did they!' smiled Willinika.

'We can collect all the rewards!' danced Nelly. 'We'll be rich!' She laughed, throwing her arms around her dad for a hug.

'Nelly?' frowned her dad, peeling a large piece of fly-encrusted paper from her cheek.

'What have you done to your face?'

'I'll tell you on the way home,' sighed Nelly.

17

'I don't care about the reward money any more,' huffed Nelly, tugging a piece of flypaper from her hair and flicking it out of the car window. 'Ring the wildlife park and the RSPCA and tell them where they can find all the lost pets. All I want to do is get home.'

'But you could collect all the reward money,' said her dad, turning the car out of the industrial estate, and back in the direction of home.

Nelly stared at her reflection in the passenger mirror. 'Not with a face like this I couldn't,' she grumped.

'It doesn't really show up that much,' fibbed her dad, slowing down for the Tom Thumb roundabout.

'Well, you noticed it!' huffed Nelly.

'But I'm your dad,' said her dad. 'Dads notice

things like that,' he bluffed.

'Just take me home will you,' sighed Nelly.

When Nelly's dad placed the house key in the door, he did so under the strict instructions not to let Asti see Nelly until she had removed all of the sticky flypaper from her body, clothing and hair.

All had gone well at first.

Asti had been distracted by her dad with tales of lost sea lions and Labradors and Nelly had managed to smuggle herself invisibly into the bathroom.

The strong soapy solution that finally detached the glue from her clothes and body ended up being an experimental combination of hand soap, shampoo, hair conditioner and bubble bath.

However, one big problem still remained.

When Nelly returned downstairs and went into the lounge, she entered the room in a rather eccentric way.

'NELLY'S GOT A TAN!' screamed Asti, pointing to Nelly's face as she sidled across the room towards an armchair that she seldom chose to sit on.

'Why's Nelly's face all tanned?' protested Asti. 'It's not fair! Now she's going to be browner than me when we go to the school disco on Monday!'

It was true. Unbeknown to Nelly, the ultraviolet lighting in the Ultravores' home had indeed given her face a rather impressive tan.

Well half-tan.

The problem was that Nelly had spent most of her time at the Ultravores' home with one cheek stuck to the curtains.

'Nelly's only got half a tan!' squealed Asti, scuttling around Nelly's armchair for a closer look. 'Look, Mum, look, Dad! Half of Nelly's face is brown and half of Nelly's face is white!'

Nelly groaned and buried her face in a cushion. One nightmare had ended and another was about to begin.

How ultra disastrous was that?

THE
RiMES
AT THE LiMES

1

With only thirty-six hours available for her ultraviolet tan to fade, Nelly found herself with no option but to leave for school on Monday morning with half a tanned face.

Not surprisingly, Asti led the ridicule from the moment Nelly stepped through the school gates.

'Look at Nelly, everyone!' she squawked. 'Look at her face! Half of it is white and half of it is brown! She looks like a white and brown . . . er . . . a white and brown kind of stripy person!'

'Is that the best you can do?' sighed Nelly, bracing herself for much worse to come.

'She looks like a freak!' shrieked Natalie Dupré, swinging her school bag on to her back and barging through a circle of onlookers.

'Yes!' leered Asti, bolstered by the spitefulness of her best friend. 'She looks like a freak! And I'll tell you why too! Because do you know what she's been doing?'

Natalie and the gathering crowd of school children drew closer and stared like a pack of inquisitive jackals.

'She's been babysitting for FREAKS! Real monster freaks!'

Nelly lowered her school bag to the ground and defiantly returned each stare in turn.

'She's been touching real monsters!' cackled Asti. 'She's been going to real monsters' houses and letting little monster freaks sit on her lap and everything! And now look what's happened! She's caught the plague! A real monster plague. Look, see her face, that's a plague that is, it's called monsteritis and if you touch her you'll turn into a monster yourself!'

The circle of school shoes stepped back at the mention of the word 'plague' and then parted as the lone figure of a boy stepped into the circle.

'What's up, Nell?' he said with concern.

Nelly looked up and acknowledged his arrival

with an awkward half-smile. It was her wish-he-was-kind-of-my-boyfriend, Craig.

'DON'T KISS HER, WHATEVER YOU DO!' screeched Asti, throwing her arms up in the air. 'You'll grow six heads if you kiss her!'

Craig's eyes darted from the extraordinary two-tone complexion of Nelly's face and then turned

contemptuously towards Asti.

'Didn't you know she'd like to kiss you?' Asti gurned. 'Haven't you told Craig you fancy him, Nellsmell?' she cackled. 'Haven't you told him how much you'd like to SNOG HIM? WELL, HE WON'T WANT TO SNOG YOU NOW!!!'

Nelly boiled with molten embarrassment as the circle of onlookers rocked with laughter. Being taunted by a bunch of small-minded morons was no problem for Nelly at all, but being humiliated by her sister in front of Craig Parmenter was unbearable.

'Why don't you lot crawl back to your holes?' Craig said with a glare, hooking his arm through Nelly's and leading her out of the fray. 'And why don't you book yourself into a clinic, Astilbe,' he growled, barging through and past Nelly's sister as though she wasn't there. 'Ask them for a personality transplant.'

The leer on Asti's face slipped momentarily and then returned with an extravavagant flap of both arms.

'UUURRGGGHHHH!' she squawked. 'Look,

Craig Parmenter's touched Nelly! Now he'll get monsteritis too!'

A chorus of laughter ballooned from the school gates and then floated in rises and falls towards the morning assembly hall.

'Who needs enemies with sisters like that,' said Craig, slipping his arm out from Nelly's and dropping it by his side.

'I know,' sighed Nelly, kind of wishing he'd kept it where it was.

'What happened to your face?' asked Craig, kicking a small stone in the direction of the main building.

'I had a bit of an accident when I was monster sitting at the weekend,' said Nelly. 'The monsters were called Ultravores, and there were ultraviolet lights everywhere.'

'Cool,' said Craig.

'Really?' asked Nelly.

'Really,' nodded Craig.

The two friends continued in silence for a few more steps, until Nelly's vanity finally got the better of her.

'Does my face really look that bad?' she stammered.

'It depends where I'm standing,' smiled Craig. 'From one side you look normal, from the other side you like you've been on a six-week holiday to Barbados!'

'And from front on?' laughed Nelly, ignoring stares from a gauntlet of fourth-formers.

'Er, from front on you look like a half-toasted teacake!' laughed Craig.

Nelly stopped dead in her tracks, slipped the strap from her shoulder and swung her school bag into the middle of Craig's back.

'I DO NOT!' she laughed.

'OK!' chuckled Craig, preparing to defend himself with his own bag. 'Let's just say you look a bit weird!'

With a truce called, the two friends continued on their way.

'Maybe I am a bit weird,' smiled Nelly. 'How many people do you know that would dare go monster sitting?'

'I would,' said Craig, using the toe of his boot

to launch another stone in the direction of the staff car park.

'Really?' said Nelly.

'Really,' said Craig.

'Cool,' said Nelly.

'Are you going to the school disco tonight?' asked Craig.

'I haven't made up my mind' said Nelly as they approached the steps leading into the main school building. 'I think I'll see how today goes.'

'I think you should,' said Craig.

'Really?' asked Nelly.

'Really,' said Craig.

'Scool!' thought Nelly, her mind on two things at once.

2

School it was. Cool it wasn't. Giggles, jokes, leers and laughter followed Nelly wherever her timetable took her. Her two-tone face was the topic of the day for just about every pupil in her year, and by the time the school bell rang at the end of the day, she was seething with fury.

Chants of 'Plague Face!' had followed her home. Orchestrated by Asti. Chants of 'Freak Lover' had followed her up the garden path. Orchestrated by Asti. And chants of Monsteritis Plaguey Face Freak Lover had followed her all the way up the stairs to her bedroom. Courtesy of Asti.

If Nelly had had a machine gun concealed inside her lime-green hot-water bottle instead of a monster sitting notebook, she would have taken it out there and then and filled her sister full of bullets.

Instead, she slammed the door of her bedroom, locked the door with a sharp twist of the key and collapsed on to her bed.

It had been the worst day of her life.

With a monster sigh, she slipped her hands behind her head and stared miserably up at the ceiling. The word was out. Her secret was no longer a secret. Everyone but everyone knew she was a monster sitter now. Thanks and no thanks to Asti.

A jumble of different thoughts avalanched through her mind. Why shouldn't she be a monster sitter? Some of the nicest 'people' she'd ever met were monsters. So what if she had half a tanned face? Half a tan was better than no tan at all. Where could she buy a machine gun, if she really wanted to get hold of one? Did Craig really want her to go to the school disco? Could she bear going back to the school that evening? Could she bear going back to the school ever again? Maybe she could change schools. Maybe hand grenades were cheaper than machine guns. Did Craig like her? Did Craig like her a lot?

Would Craig kind of be her boyfriend? Would everyone make fun of her at the disco? Would the disco lighting hide her two-tone face? Would the DJ keep playing the 'Monster Mash'?

Nelly closed her eyes tight and then swept the avalanche of thoughts away with an imaginary snow shovel.

'I AM going to go to the disco tonight!' she determined. 'I'm going to show Asti. I'm going to show Natalie Dupré. I'm going to show everyone!'

Her eyes opened to reveal a steely glint of determination.

'Nothing and no one phases Nelly the Monster Sitter!'

She slipped her palms out from under her head and pushed herself up from the bed.

Nelly the schoolgirl turned defiantly towards the door of her wardrobe. It was less than blessed with disco outfits.

'Cream blouse and new jeans!' she smiled.

Nelly the Monster Sitter turned defiantly towards her monster sitting diary. Only yesterday she had pencilled in her next appointment.

'Wednesday six o'clock the Rimes at the Limes!' She smiled. 'The Rimes at the Limes,' she conjured, 'The Rimes at the Limes!' What a strange telephone conversation that had been!

'I'll need to brush up on my poetry at school tomorrow,' she thought with a smile, unlocking the door of her bedroom and making her way to the bathroom.

'Surprise, surprise,' she sighed. The bathroom was occupied.

'I cannot believe you went to school today with a face like that!' said Asti, applying a thin line of mascara to each of her eyes in turn.

'And I can't believe you told Craig Parmenter I fancied him!' growled Nelly.

'Well, it's true, isn't it?' said Asti, searching through her make-up bag for some disco-perfect blusher. 'I've probably done you a favour.'

'AND you told the whole school I go monster sitting!' snapped Nelly.

'I didn't tell the whole school!' smirked Asti. 'I told the whole year.'

'Well, the whole school seems to know!' said

Nelly, looking around the bathroom for a suitable murder weapon.

'And so they should.' Asti puckered her lips in front of the numor. 'We don't want them catching your plague.'

'You're the only disease around here,' fumed Nelly.

Asti lowered her lipstick and stared admiringly at her own reflection.

'Er . . . excuse me,' she said. 'Have you looked in the mirror recently?'

Nelly looked down at the bathroom scales. She could probably do a good job of bashing her sister's brains out with them. Trouble is, bit of a tricky murder weapon to dispose of, bathroom scales.

'Just hurry up, will you!' growled Nelly, wheeling round and pointing herself back in the direction of her bedroom. 'I want to get ready too.'

Asti turned away from the bathroom mirror and stared at the empty doorway in astonishment.

'You're not going to the school disco with a face like THAT!' she gasped.

'I AM!' shouted Nelly.

'But you CAN'T!' squealed Asti.

'Watch me!' shouted Nelly, with a slam of her bedroom door.

3

At seven o'clock that evening, the doors of Lowbridge High School reopened and the normally spiritless assembly hall exploded with disco strobing and thump thump bass.

Asti was one of the first through the school gates.

Having arrived home from school at half past three, it had taken her three and a quarter solid hours to get ready. She had left towels on the floor, the flannel in the bath, the soap in the plughole, her make-up on every surface available, and the empty packet from her nail extensions on the hallway landing.

At a quarter to seven she had left for the disco, leaving Nelly to pick her way through the carnage.

'I didn't think Nelly would come!' giggled Natalie Dupré, catching up Asti with she entered the school building, and sidling up to her in the shortest skirt she was allowed to leave her house in. 'Not with a face like that!'

'Oh, she's coming all right,' shuddered Asti. 'She might not be here yet, but she's coming.'

Natalie ran her tongue across her dental brace and then stared blankly at the doorway to the disco.

'But she's got the plague,' she gasped. 'People can't go to a school disco with the plague!'

'Nelly's not normal people,' said Asti.

She paused for a moment to redo her make-up, and then slipped her compact mirror back into her bag.

'Go and see if Darren Leadbetter is here yet,' said Asti, with a nod in the direction of the assembly hall door.

'Are you going to ask him out?' grinned Natalie, fumbling around in her own clutch bag in search of her disco ticket.

'No!' laughed Asti. 'He's going to ask ME out!'

Natalie wiggled to the door on her non-school-regulation heels, and then flapped her hands at Asti.

'He's there!' she mouthed excitedly.

Asti pulled her lipstick from her clutch bag again, and re-did her lips.

'You lucky lucky boy, Darren,' she purred, flipping open her compact mirror and admiring

her reflection once again. 'Come to Asti.' She smiled, planted a kiss on her disco ticket and tottered through the disco entrance.

'Good evening, Natalie, good evening, Astilbe,' said Mr Bovingdon, the PE teacher, marking the backs of each girl's hand with a printing stamp.

Asti looked down at the the smudge of blue ink and shuddered. It clashed horribly with her nail extensions.

'There he is!' said Natalie, tugging Asti's arm. 'Look, he's over there with Colin Lampton and Josh Waites!'

Asti threw a covert glance across to the tables that lined the far wall of the darkened assembly hall, and then dragged Natalie by the elbow in the direction of the fizzy drinks.

'Don't look at them!' she whispered. 'They'll think we're interested.'

'We are interested, aren't we?' said Natalie, a little confused.

'Yes,' said Asti, swapping some money for a cherry Coke, 'but we don't want them to know that. We need to play hard to get.'

Natalie opened her own bag and paid for an orange Fanta.

'Where shall we sit?' she said, scanning the three remaining perimeter walls of the disco hall.

'Over there!' said Asti, pointing to the stage. 'We'll sit on the stage and wait for some more girls to arrive.'

The disco was quick to fill up, and a steady stream of non-regulation high heels, non-regulation make-up and non-regulation short skirts had soon joined Asti and Natalie on the lip of the school stage.

'Is Darren still there?' said Asti, trying to look without looking.

'I can't see,' said Natalie, bobbing her head up and down. 'Yes, he is! He's talking to Craig Parmenter!'

Asti's face starched.

'UURRRGGHHH!' squeaked Natalie, lowering her Fanta bottle from her lips. 'Craig Parmenter touched Nelly this morning! You don't think he'll give Darren Leadbetter the plague too, do you? I mean, if you kiss Darren Leadbetter and he's got the plague your lips might fall off or something!'

Asti squinted up at the disco lights and sighed. 'It's not a real plague, Natalie, there's no such thing as monsteritis in real life. I just made it up.'

Natalies mouth opened and then shut. 'So Nelly's not going to sprout six noses?'

'No,' sighed Asti

'Or grow another head?'

'No,' sighed Asti.

'And she won't get duck webbing growing between her toes?'

'No, Natalie. I made that up too,' sighed Asti. 'It was a JOKE!'

'I knew that,' fibbed Natalie. 'Do you want another cherry Coke?'

Asti nodded and then moved on to the dance floor for a closer look at Darren Leadbetter. Sure enough he was sitting at a table with his mates, talking to Craig Parmenter. But why was he talking to Craig? And more importantly what were they saying?

Asti danced her way sideways across the floor,

and drew as close to the boys' table as she could without looking obvious.

All ears but no eyes, she strained to decipher what they were saying above the music, but it was hopeless.

'ASTI!' squawked a familiarly excitable voice.

Asti turned back in the direction of the stage to find a bottle of cherry Coke dangling in front of her face.

'NELLY'S ARRIVED!' said Natalie. 'Honest to God! Nelly's just come though the door!'

4

Asti bobbed and weaved her eyeline through a sea of dancing heads, and then fastened her sights like a harpoon on her sister's ponytail and scrunchy.

To her delight, Nelly was making her way across the dance floor to the exact same table where Craig and Darren were sitting. Heads turned and stared all the way as she threaded and pushed her two-tone way through.

'Time for some fun!' thought Asti, delaying her pounce until the precise moment her sister arrived at the table.

'Nellsmell!' she cackled, handing her cherry Coke back to Natalie and then striding up to where the circle of boys were sitting. 'How's the plague treating you?' she snorted, placing her hands squarely on her sister's shoulders and rotating her in all directions for all to see.

'Get lost,' said Nelly, wrenching her shoulders free from her sister's grasp.

Asti threw a come-and-get-me glance in the direction of Darren Leadbetter and then continued her verbal onslaught.

'Don't worry, boys, it's not the plague really!' she piped, running her palm down the side of Nelly's cheek. 'This half of her face is just the side that the monsters sucked her blood out!'

Natalie fluttered her eyelashes at Josh Waites and then added her two penny worth. 'Yes, that's where they sucked half her blood out, which means . . . she's only got half her blood!'

Nelly brushed Asti's hand away and looked downheartedly at Craig. 'I said get lost, Asti,' she growled.

'Sorry, sis,' said Asti. 'Did I smudge your make-up? Oh no, I forgot. You don't wear make-up, do you!' she shrieked. 'But then there isn't a make-up in the world that could do anything for a FACE LIKE THAT!' she hooted.

Nelly wilted.

Natalie moved in with a wave of the cherry Coke bottle.

'MAYBE YOU SHOULD HAVE BOUGHT SOME BROWN PAINT AND PAINTED THE WHITE HALF OF YOUR FACE WITH IT!' she shrieked.

'OR SOME WHITE PAINT AND PAINTED THE BROWN HALF OF YOUR FACE WITH THAT!' cackled Asti.

'OR . . .' added Natalie, keen to keep striking while the iron was hot, but suddenly finding herself unable to develop the white – brown theme any further.

'OR JUST THROWN YOURSELF UNDER A BUS!' laughed Asti.

Nelly stood and suffered in silence, as her sister threw a wide grin around all the boys that were seated around the table.

No one was smiling though.

Except Asti and Natalie.

'Get lost, Astilbe,' said Craig, standing up and offering Nelly his chair.

Nelly lifted her head and stared at the

empty seat in astonishment.

'Yeah, you heard your sister, get lost the both of you,' said Darren Leadbetter, dismissing Asti's presence with a contemptuous curl of his lip.

Asti's grin fell from her face and shattered like plate glass on the disco floor.

Nelly's eyes darted downwards to the seat that Craig had vacated for her and then upwards to the smile that was waiting for her. With a glare at her sister, she accepted the boys' invitation to join them.

Asti's face crumpled with envy and then wheeled away across the disco floor.

'Come on, Natalie,' she wavered. 'We're obviously not wanted around here!'

'Do you want some more of your cherry Coke?' bleated Natalie, scampering across the disco floor with her arm outstretched.

'NO I DON'T!' stomped Asti.

Nelly watched as the back of her sister's disco top disappeared into the crowd and then turned to Craig with a smile.

'Thanks,' she said.

'No problem,' he shrugged.

'No really, I owe you,' said Nelly, secretly trying to develop the bond that seemed to be growing between them.

'Will you tell us all about monster sitting?' he asked.

Nelly looked around the table at a circle of admiring eyes.

'Will you buy me a Fanta?' smiled Nelly.

'And some crisps if you like!' he laughed.

'Then I'll tell you about monster sitting!' laughed Nelly.

5

For the entire duration of the disco, Nelly held court with the boys like King Arthur before the Knights of the Round Table. To her astonishment and thinly disguised pleasure, they were riveted by all of the monster sitting stories she had to tell.

Each tale she told drew her listeners' elbows a little further across the table. Each description she gave widened her audience's eyes a little wider. At all times, she was careful not to give too much away. For Nelly, the privacy of her monsters remained paramount. No addresses were disclosed and no telephone numbers were ever mentioned.

'You are totally the coolest person in the school by a mile,' said Darren Leadbetter, offering Nelly a swig of his shandy Bass.

'REALLY?!' laughed Nelly, blushing red on

even the brown half of her face.

She wasn't used to compliments like that, especially from totally the best-looking boy in the school by a mile!

Nelly popped a cheese and onion crisp in her mouth and glanced upwards to where totally the nicest boy in the school by a mile was standing.

'Darren's right,' smiled Craig. 'What you're doing is really cool.'

'I don't do it to be cool,' said Nelly, with an exchange of twinkles. 'I just think it's nice to help monsters out. After all how would you like to be stuck indoors all the time?'

Her circle of admirers nodded and then waited eagerly for the next instalment.

'What kind of monsters are you monster sitting next?' asked Craig, nudging her shoulder with his hip in the hope of sharing her chair.

Nelly needed no encouraging and budged over to make room.

'Rimes.' She smiled as Craig joined her on the chair. 'They phoned me up on Sunday when I was doing my homework.'

'I'd much rather go monster sitting than do homework,' sighed Josh Waites.

'You'd rather do anything than do homework!' smiled Craig, making himself as comfortable as he could.

'It was one of the strangest phone calls I've ever had,' continued Nelly with another munch of her crisps.

'Whhhhhhyyyy?' chorused the circle of boys.

'The clue's in the name,' smiled Nelly. 'They're called the Rimes because they rhyme everything!'

All of the eyebrows around the table rose like a Mexican wave.

'Every time they say something they say it in rhyme!' reiterated Nelly.

'What, EVERYTHING they say?' asked Darren.

'*That is their way!*' rhymed Nelly with a chuckle.

'And you're going to their house?' asked Josh.

'*I'm a girl not a mouse!*' rhymed Nelly playfully.

Collin Lampton drained the remaining drops from his shandy Bass bottle and then asked the question that was on all of the boys' minds.

'What do Rimes look like?' he probed.

'I don't know yet!' smiled Nelly. 'That's the best bit about getting a phone call from a monster you don't know. You have to guess from their voice what they are going to look like when they open their front door for the first time. They could be scaly, hairy, gungy, spiky, you just never really know.'

'What did they sound like?' asked Darren.

'Poetic!' laughed Nelly.

The boys exchanged blank glances around the table. They couldn't even begin to guess what a poetic monster would look like.

'My guess is they'll be scaly,' smiled Nelly. 'I'm seeing them on Wednesday, so I'll be able to tell you on Thursday!'

The circle of friends smiled and then blinked rapidly as the darkness of the disco hall reverted to the brightness of an assembly hall.

The disco had ended, the lights were back on, the DJ was packing up and they had barely left their seats.

'Respect,' said Darren Leadbetter leaning across the table and holding out his knuckle.

Nelly clenched her fist and tapped his knuckle with hers. 'It's been fun!' she smiled.

'Can I walk you home?' said Craig, plonking his empty bottle on to the table and vacating his half of the chair.

'I wish!' beamed Nelly, 'but my mum will be waiting outside in the car.'

'I'll see you tomorrow then,' smiled Craig. '. . . if you like,' he added.

'I do like!' beamed Nelly. 'I like very much!'

As Craig and the boys turned to leave, Nelly peered across the emptying dance floor to see if Asti was waiting for her by the entrance.

If she was, she couldn't see her.

Asti in fact had left the disco an hour early and had been sitting in the car park with a face like a mutant turnip.

If Nelly had had half a mind to buy a machine gun and some grenades earlier, there were no limits to the weaponry that Asti was planning to spend her Christmas money on.

'I'll kill her!' Asti muttered under her breath, as her mum drew up in the car park and opened the Maestro door. 'She's turned everyone against me! Including Darren Leadbetter! I will absolutely kill her!'

'Did you have a nice time?' asked Mum innocently as Asti slumped into the front seat of the car.

'NO, I DIDN'T!' screeched Asti, thumping the dashboard so hard the car radio jumped channels.'

'It was rubbish! And it's all Nelly's FAULT!'

'Her mum frowned, beginning to wish she'd harangued her husband into picking the girls up instead.

'Hiya!' beamed Nelly, dropping her two-tone face to driver level and greeting her mum with a cheery wave. 'Have you been waiting long?'

Nelly's mum smiled back, relieved to be on the receiving end of some politeness.

'Did YOU have a nice time?' she ventured hopefully as Nelly buckled up in the back.

'I had a brilliant time, thanks,' said Nelly, daggering the back of Asti's head with a triumphant glare. 'I had the best time EVER!'

'You're dead,' muttered Asti, staring demonically across the bonnets of the cars as they filed their way out of the school car park.

'Really!' smiled Nelly, clamping her thumb and forefinger to her wrist. 'This feels like a pulse to me!'

6

It was Asti's pulse that became the most erratic over the next two days. Not only had she been spurned by Darren Leadbetter, not only had she had to watch Nelly and Craig Parmenter become an item, but, and this was the killer, but her nauseating, ponytail-wearing, fashionless freak of a sister had become the coolest person in school. Without make-up, without crispbreads, even without body piercings, Nelly-the-Monster-Sitter-Morton had suddenly become the person that everyone suddenly wanted to be and know.

Despite her new-found celebrity, Nelly had kept her regulation school shoes firmly on the ground. In fact all of her break times during Tuesday and Wednesday had been spent reading rhyming couplets in the school library.

By the time she ambled out of the school gate

with Craig Parmenter she was brimful of the poetry of Wordsworth and Keats.

'I'm seeing the Rimes tonight!' Nelly smiled, oblivious to the fact that Asti was most likely lying on the school roof with a sniper rifle.

'I'd come with you, if you'd let me,' said Craig, 'only poetry isn't really my thing!'

'Maybe next time,' said Nelly. 'It's better you don't come to the Rimes: in fact I couldn't let you come with me to the Rimes.'

'Why's that?' asked Craig, more than a little intrigued.

'Well,' said Nelly with a nibble of her lip. 'Looking after the Rimes is going to be a bit trickier than I let on at the disco.'

'Go on?' urged Craig hooking his school bag over his head.

'Well,' continued Nelly, 'you know I said the Rimes speak in rhyme?'

'Yes,' said Craig.

'Well, when you speak to them you have to speak in rhyme too.'

Craig continued in silence for the next few paces.

'I mean HAVE TO,' stressed Nelly.

'Or what?' asked Craig, slowing almost to a halt.

'Or . . . they . . . er . . . die,' winced Nelly. 'Well, maybe they don't die, maybe they just go into a coma or something, but they definitely fall unconscious, they told me.'

'How do you know? What did they say to you?' gasped Craig, now more than a little intrigued.

Nelly frowned as she tried to replay the exact conversation she had had with the Rimes, through her head.

'They said something like this.' She coughed.

'Please come and visit
Our home is exquisite.
But Nelly beware
You must take great care
To speak like we do,
Your whole visit through.
It's crucial you rhyme
What you say every time.
The instant you fail

Our faces will pale
Our heart beats will stop
To the floor we will drop.'

Craig tugged Nelly to an abrupt halt.

'Nelly, that's dangerous!' he gasped. 'What if you can't think of a rhyme? What will happen then?'

'I'll be fine,' smiled Nelly. 'They only need me to visit for about an hour and I've been practising non-stop since Sunday. I'm sure I can think up enough rhymes in an hour.'

'Don't tell me,' sighed Craig. '*You're a poet and didn't know it!*'

'I certainly am,
Or my name is Sam!' said Nelly.

'That's not poetry, it's terrible!' laughed Craig.

'It might be terrible but it still rhymed, didn't it!' said Nelly, leading the way across the road and into Floss Street.

'Are you still not talking to Asti?' Craig asked, glancing further up the street just in time to see Nelly's sister hurry around the corner into Glee Gardens.

'She hates me,' said Nelly.

'Do you hate her?' asked Craig.

'Kind of,' said Nelly, 'but I can't *hate her* hate her, she's my sister.'

'Same with me and my brother,' said Craig.

'He's only SIX!' laughed Nelly.

'He can still be a pain though,' replied Craig.

'Asti's a different kind of pain, I promise you,' said Nelly wryly.

'Did you know Darren fancies her?' asked Craig.

Nelly, stopped dead in her tracks. 'But he told her to get lost at the disco.'

'He did that for you,' said Craig. 'Well, me actually.'

Nelly stared up the road in the direction of Glee Gardens. What would Asti give to know that Darren Leadbetter fancied her!

'Are you going to tell her?' asked Craig.

'I would if she stopped teasing me.' She smiled.

'Good luck at the Rimes' tonight,' said Craig, waving goodbye and then cutting right into Fountain Street. 'Tell me all about it tomorrow!'

'*Parting is such sweet sorrow!*' swooned Nelly,

clasping her hand dramatically to her chest.

'Aha! You ARE a poet!' shouted Craig from the other side of the road.

'*Let's hope I don't blow it!*' waved Nelly.

7

No one had been exactly sure why Asti had returned home from school at lunchtime earlier that day, or why instead of eating her crispbreads she had swallowed a cocktail of Instant Whip, beef stock cubes and lemon juice.

Only one thing was certain. She had returned to school in the afternoon with a tummy full of gurgles, and run home at the end of the day with . . . well the runs.

'I think she was trying to kill herself,' said Nelly, pegging her nose with her fingers as she walked past the lavatory door. 'Darren Leadbetter told her to get lost at the school disco.'

'Of course I wasn't trying to kill myself!' squawked Asti, rushing from her bedroom door in the direction of the loo. 'It was a cry for help!'

Nelly's mum sighed. Ever since the night of the school disco, Asti's mood had darkened beyond reason. She had rarely come out of her room and had been surviving on little more than a diet of cottage cheese and teen mags.

'A cry for help!' she laughed. 'You try keeping a house tidy twenty-four hours a day, seven days a week, you try having dinner on the table every night, AND remembering to water the aloe vera. I'm the one that needs the help around here!'

'I hate you!' screamed Asti, rushing into the bathroom and slamming the door behind her. 'I hate you all!'

Nelly looked at her mum and then smiled as the bathroom erupted with the rather indelicate sounds of a bottom out of control.

'I've never known anything so ridiculous in my life!' growled her mum. 'First she wants to pierce herself full of holes, then she won't eat properly, now she's gorging herself on Instant Whip mixed up with goodness knows what else. And all over a BOY!'

'He IS the best-looking boy in the school,' said Nelly rather charitably.

'Well, your father wasn't a bad looker either, when I met him, but you wouldn't have found me stabbing myself with needles or poisoning myself with home-made slop, just to catch his eye.'

Nelly tried to imagine her dad as a teenager, but even for a girl with her imagination it was a thought too far.

'What's aloe vera?' she asked.

'It's the cactussy-looking plant on the window ledge in the kitchen,' said her mum. 'The stuff inside its leaves is good for your skin, but if you don't water it enough the leaves start to shrivel.'

'Next time I see it I'll water it,' said Nelly with a smile, heading for her bedroom to get changed out of her school uniform.

'Make sure you don't OVERwater it!' said her mum. 'Too much water is just as bad as no water at all.'

Nelly pulled her school tie from her neck and sighed. Under the circumstances it would probably be better if her mum continued to deal with the aloe vera.

'Can I have dinner late tonight?' Nelly shouted, entering her bedroom and glancing at her monster sitting diary. 'I'm monster sitting for the Rimes at six!'

'Suits me fine!' said her mum, returning downstairs and leaving Asti to deal with her squits. 'I haven't had time to get anything out of the freezer yet anyway.'

'That makes a change!' mumbled Nelly, closing her bedroom door and beelining for the sardine T-shirt that was hanging in her wardrobe.

'I hate you!' screamed Asti, thumping Nelly's bedroom door with her fist on her way back to her own bedroom.

'What is she like!' sighed Nelly, pulling her green jeans from a hanger. 'More importantly, what will the Rimes be like too?'

She grinned.

8

'I'll take you!' said Nelly's dad, plucking the car keys from his pocket, and U-turning out of the front door the instant he had stepped in from work.

If there was one thing living with three females had taught him, it was to escape from the house the instant he sensed trouble.

And sense trouble he did.

There was a chill about the house.

In fact Asti's frosty mood was drifting down the stairs like dry ice.

'I'll take you monster sitting this evening!' said Nelly's dad, limping back down the driveway towards the safety of the car. 'Where do you want to go?'

'The Rimes at the Limes, please!' shouted Nelly, slapping a Post-it with the Rimes' address and telephone number on to the hallway mirror, and then jumping out of the house to catch him up.

'Barleysugar Drive,' she said, joining her dad in the car, 'near the reservoir.'

'Excellent!' said her dad, secretly relieved to be driving further afield. The longer the journey, the more time the house would have to thaw.

'Guess what those lazy ambulance drivers are planning now!' he exclaimed as the Maestro left the drive. 'A march! A march down the high street on Saturday!'

Nelly wasn't really sure what to say. After all, if the ambulance drivers were still on strike, surely they were striking for a good reason.

'Imagine the chaos that's going to cause!' exclaimed her dad. 'The entire high street is going to be closed off from two o'clock. It's an absolute disgrace!'

Nelly stayed quiet and waited for her dad's political rant to fizzle out. By the time they had reached the top of Coconut Street, he had returned to political issues closer to home.

'Is it my imagination,' he said, 'or does the house feel particularly frosty this evening?'

'It's Asti's fault,' said Nelly. 'She took an overdose of Instant Whip, lemon juice, and beef stock cubes today,' she sighed. 'She's OK, but she's got the squits big time.'

'What on earth is the matter with her at the moment?' asked her dad.

'She said it was a cry for help,' smiled Nelly. 'She's in love.'

'A cry for what? She's been reading too many magazines if you ask me,' sighed her dad. 'I don't know what sort of help those teenage magazines think they're giving, but I'd be very surprised if it extended to Instant Whip, lemon juice and beef stock cubes.'

Nelly looked out of the car window, and then leaned further over to catch a glimpse of her reflection in the wing mirror.

Four days had passed since she had been stuck to the flypaper curtains at the Ultravores'.

'Do you think my face is going back to normal?' she asked.

Nelly's dad said nothing. He was still conjuring with gastric implications of Asti's lunch.

'Dad, do you think my half-tan is fading?' Nelly asked again.

Nelly's dad returned his thoughts to the road ahead and puffed out his cheeks.

'Let's put it this way, Nelly. I think it's highly unlikely that the Rimes will have much to say about your face. You probably look quite normal to a monster!'

Nelly wasn't sure whether to take that as a compliment or not.

'Everyone at school had lots to say about it,' she sighed, scanning for purple doors along Fondant Way. 'The first day at least.'

'I'm sure they did,' said her dad. 'Schools can be the cruellest places on earth when they want to be. I remember getting my hair cut when I was your age. I hated the first day at school after a haircut. Everyone but everyone used to take the mickey. Even if it was only a trim! But by the end of the day, though, everyone had forgotten about it and moved on.'

Nelly leaned towards the wing mirror again and turned her face in either direction.

'It was a bit like that for me,' she said. 'By Tuesday most people left me alone . . . except Asti and Natalie.' She frowned.

'You surprise me,' sighed her dad. 'I do wish you and Asti got on better. Both me and your mum do. But somehow I think you were born to squabble.'

'She's the one who squabbles, not me!' said Nelly. 'She's a pea-brained loser, and I'm glad she's got the squits. In fact I hope she keeps having the squits until my tan fades. Actually, I hope she has to keep running to the loo for another six weeks AFTER my tan fades!'

'Do you know who you reminded me of then?' sighed her dad.

'Who?' asked Nelly, not sure she was going to like the answer.

'Your sister.' He tutted.

'Just drive!' humphed Nelly in disgust.

9

The reservoir area of the Montelimar Estate was about as far north as Nelly's monster sitting appointments had ever taken her. Although only minutes from the Éclair Towers Estate, it was a much posher proposition altogether.

The houses in Barleysugar Drive were large and detached. Long front gardens swept forward from the oak front doors, and immense pea-shingled driveways gave grand access to the road. The red-brick walls that fronted the pavement were topped with tall copper beech hedges. Even the bird boxes that were nailed in the front gardens had an air of des res about them.

Lime trees lined either side of the gravel driveway that was now crunching under the weight of four slightly balding Maestro tyres.

'Verrrry nice,' said Nelly's dad, swinging his eyes left across the flowerbeds towards a perfectly manicured front lawn.

'Your mum wouldn't mind living here,' he said with a nod of approval. 'As long as I did all the gardening,' he added.

Nelly glanced at her watch. It was a minute to six. 'Hurry up and park!' she said, 'or I'll be late!'

'Oh, yes,' said her dad, applying the hand brake with a wistful tug, 'I could most definitely see myself living here.'

Nelly undid her seat belt and then stayed her dad's hand as he went to unclip his own.

'You can't come with me, Dad, you'll say the wrong thing,' she frowned.

'I beg your pardon!' protested her dad. 'I'm very good with monsters, I'll have you know. I've met the Muggots and the Huffaluks, and now the Ultravores. Mr Pellion and I got on famously once he'd realized I wasn't you!'

Nelly smiled and then placed her hand on her dad's knee. 'Sorry, Dad, when I say you'll say the wrong thing I don't mean you'll say the wrong thing exactly, it's just that whatever you say won't rhyme.'

'Rhyme?' said Nelly's dad, loosening his grip on his belt buckle.

'It's a long story,' said Nelly. 'Just let me do this on my own, please.'

Nelly's dad did as he was asked and watched curiously through the windscreen of the Maestro as Nelly climbed out of the car and crunched across the gravel to the front porch of the house.

'*The Rimes at the Limes, the Rimes at the Limes!*' she smiled, peering back towards the Maestro.

With a glance at her watch, she pressed the porcelain doorbell and then stepped back as it greeted her with a tuneful rhyming chime.

'Don't blow it,' she whispered to herself as she waited for the door to be answered. '*Don't blow it, don't blow it! Think poet, think poet!*'

As Nelly waited for the front door to open, and a Rime to appear, all of the rhymes she had prepared and rehearsed tumbled and jumbled through her mind.

'I hope I've got enough rhymes to last an

hour,' she thought with a nibble of her lip. 'What if I forget them? What will I do then?'

Her eyes switched from the front door back to her dad. For some strange reason, he was jabbing towards the side of the house with his index finger.

Nelly looked at her watch again. It was two minutes past six. She raised her hand to ring the doorbell again and then jumped as a huge-fingered claw bristling with two sharp spikes daggered towards her from around the corner of the house.

Nelly jumped back and then blew a sigh of relief.

It was a gardening glove holding a pair of secateurs.

Nelly's eyes widened further as two furry balls appeared from around the corner of the house, attached to one body by a forked flower stalk-green neck.

'Two heads, and a V-shaped neck!' she gasped to herself. Could she remember her first rhyme, could she remember her first rhyme?

She held her breath for a moment and then beamed as the rest of its body swung into view.

Nelly stepped forward immediately and extended her arm for a handshake. With a puff of her cheeks, and a cross of her fingers she went for it.

'*Hello, my name is Nelly,*
You must be the Rimes
It's really nice to be a
guest here at the Limes!'

It was well rehearsed, boldly delivered and generously received.

'*Excellent, Nelly, thought it was you,*' chimed both furry faces at once.

'*My name is Meeta, how do you do?*'

Nelly glanced at her watch. It was 6.03. Only fifty-seven more rhyming minutes to go!

With an excited wave to her dad, she composed herself as Meeta removed the gardening gloves from the end of his hosepipe-green arms, and closed five warm sucker-tipped fingers around hers.

Nelly's dad stared agog at the monster that was greeting his daughter, and then slipped the Maestro into reverse gear.

'Rather her than me,' he muttered, reversing out of the lime-tree-lined drive with a wave.

'6.04,' thought Nelly scrutinizing her wrist as the dial of her watch face bounced up and down with the handshake. 'Four minutes gone already, and I've only used up one rhyme!'

The monster that was shaking her hand was a strange one indeed. Its heads had the look of cheerleader pompoms, and its necks the bend of boy-racer car aerials. The bumblebee stripe of its faces hooped the velveteen of its arms and legs too, and yet there was even more to its appearance than first met the eye.

For it danced! Whenever it spoke, it danced!

'*Come on, Nelly, please follow me,*' smiled Meeta, his bumblebee-striped legs springing from the floor like a puppet ballerina.

'*We're in the back garden, enjoying our tea.*'

Nelly responded with a smile and a rhymeless nod. She was still building herself up for rhyme

number two, and wanted to get it word perfect.

'Here goes!' she thought, withdrawing her hand politely from the handshake.

'*Lovely weather for this time of year,*' she beamed. '*Even hotter tomorrow, from what I hear!*'

Meeta smiled with both faces, and blinked up at the evening sun.

'*Yes, the weather's been kind, and looks set to last*

But you never can trust a weather forecast!'

'He's good,' thought Nelly, marvelling at the ease with which rhymes just tripped from Meeta's tongues.

'*Follow me, Nelly,*' danced Meeta.
'*It's time for some fun,*
Come and meet Shimma,
Our dear little one!'

With her mind already planning the delivery of rhyme number three, Nelly stepped down from the front doorstep and followed Meeta around the corner of the house.

The crunch of Nelly's trainers on the pea-shingle driveway brought both mother and daughter running excitedly to the back gate.

'It's her, look it's Nelly! She's coming with Dad!
She's here, Mum, she's here! I'm EVER SO glad!'

Nelly peered through the green V of Meeta's neck and waved in the direction of the back garden gate. A pair of small but hugely excitable pompom heads were bouncing up and down behind the gate, trying to catch a better glimpse of her.

'*Nelly meet Shimma,*' laughed Meeta with a wave of the secateurs, '*and my dear wife Cavorta.*

'*No prizes for guessing which one is my daughter!*'

Nelly extended both hands over the top of the wooden gate, and greeted both mother and daughter with a double handshake and smile. There was nothing for it. It was time for rhyme number three.

'Thanks for inviting me, may I come in?

I love meeting monsters, just look at my grin!'

Not bad, not great, and undoubtedly the least classic of Nelly's rhymes so far, but nevertheless it produced six velvet-faced grins in response.

'This is going well!' thought Nelly, her confidence beginning to rise.

Cavorta's green sucker-tipped fingers lifted the latch of the back gate and then beckoned Nelly to step through and into the back garden.

And what a back garden it was.

Concealed from the driveway by a heavily flowering trellis, the Rimes' back garden was a wonder to behold.

Exotic reds, golds and yellows spilled from every border like floral lava. Silver-leafed grass gilded the manicured lawn.

In the middle of the lawn, concentric rings of golden bedding plants radiated in geometric circles towards the curve of a crescent-shaped patio.

But it was the four corners of the garden that stole the show.

For in each of the four corners of the back garden stood a Rime-figured statue. Towering perhaps four metres high from circular marble plinths, each two-headed, double swan-necked marble sculpture graced the garden with a classically striking dance pose.

'Posh or what!' thought Nelly, walking stiff-legged in the direction of the patio.

But posh was about to go gosh. For the instant Nelly placed her bottom on a seat at the garden table the statue in the far left-hand corner of the garden began to move! Dance, in fact, to a melody that had started to tinkle softly from deep inside the marble plinth.

It was like watching a giant two-headed ballerina on the top of a marble musical box!

The instant Meeta, Cavorta and Shimma became seated the three remaining statues sprang to life too.

'Seat-activated,' thought Nelly, careful not to utter words that she couldn't possibly rhyme. 'The moment you sit on a garden seat, a statue starts to play!'

Shimma clapped her hands excitedly and beamed at her furry-faced parents.

'Nelly likes our statues, I told you that she would!

I said she would, I said she would, I knew she'd think they're good!'

Nelly smiled across the garden table, opened her mouth to speak and then closed it again. None of the rhymes she had rehearsed had made any allowance for musical statues.

She raised her finger for a cautionary moment, smiled, and then thought long and hard about her reply. Shimma, Cavorta and Meeta waited patiently for the right words to come.

'Ahem,' said Nelly, eventually clearing her throat.

'Yes, I do love your statues, I think they're really nifty!

If my garden had the space I'd like to take home fifty!'

A fluted chuckle floated from the Rimes' velveteen mouths, and a look of congratulations sparkled from each eye. Cavorta leaned over from her garden seat and patted Nelly on the knee.

'Bravo, Nelly, extremely well done!

Bellissimo, fantastico, let's have another one!'

Nelly gulped, placed her hand on top of Cavorta's and then furrowed her brow once again. There was a pause. Some facial twitches. And then a stroke of poetic genius.

'Thank you for inviting me, it's really nice to visit.

Your house is a dream home, and your garden is exquisite!'

Well, if the Rimes were impressed before, they were bowled over now. Even Nelly was quite taken aback by the accomplishment of her last rhyme.

'Thank you, Wordsworth, thank you, Keats! Thank you, Byron, thank you, Yeats!' she thought to herself as the Rimes began chattering excitedly amongst themselves.

As the soft spherical bobbles of their heads bounced and nodded before her, Nelly seized the chance to take a close-up look at her surroundings.

The golden garden table that she was sitting at was littered with the leftovers from the Rimes' afternoon tea. There were no teacups as such, instead clear Perspex test tubes lay scattered on the table, with the dregs of a golden honeyed liquid left inside. There was no evidence of clotted cream and scones either, in fact the residual crumbs that remained on the three shallow silver plates were gilled pink like the underside of a mushroom.

Nelly turned her attention to Shimma. The bumblebee pattern of her velvet legs, arms and heads was banded with soft stripes of cream rather than the deep orange stripes of her parents. She was an excitable little thing, all buzz and no wings. Barely a metre tall, her tiptoed feet criss-crossed and cross-crissed comically off the ground as she sat and chatted excitedly with her parents.

Nelly looked at her watch. It was almost a quarter past six, which was good in one way, for if she was only needed for an hour she only had forty-five minutes left to keep up her rhyming. However, and it was a big however, if Meeta and Cavorta didn't leave the house soon, there wouldn't be any time left for them to go anywhere!

She waited for the Rimes' chitter-chatter to subside and then boldly opened another conversation with her most ambitious rhyme yet.

'I think it's time for me to stay
And time for you to go.
It's time for me to monster sit
That's what I do, you know!
The two of us will have some fun
We'll laugh and play and smile.
So go and have some fun yourself
We'll see you in a while.'

Meeta and Cavorta smiled at each other and then rose excitedly from the table. Nelly puffed out her chest with pride. At this rate she was going to become a contender for the Nobel poetry prize.

'*Come, I have a secret, join me over here!*' Meeta danced as he spoke, motioning Nelly to join him in the corner of the garden where one of only two musical statues were now still playing. '*To tell you where we're going, I must whisper in your ear.*'

Nelly lifted her bottom from her garden seat bringing a third statue to a halt.

'Seat-activated!' thought Nelly, striding across the lawn to the corner where Meeta was waiting. 'Boy would Mum and Dad like those!'

As she stepped into the dappled evening light of the leafy garden corner, a pair of symmetrical smiles broke across the orange bands of Meeta's furry faces.

Nelly drew close but was pulled even closer still by one of Meeta's long green velveteen arms.

Nelly's cheek began to tickle as his velvet lips came closer to her ear.

'Next week is Shimma's birthday,' Meeta whispered,
'That's why we've asked you round,
Her present will be something we

can plant into the ground.
For Nature is a Rime's best friend
For many different reasons.
The rhythm of the falling rain,
The cycle of of the seasons.
The more our garden comes to life,
The more she'll blossom too.
Shimma is the inspiration
For everything we do.
She is our garden princess
We couldn't love her more.
We'd love to plant her something
She hasn't seen before.
Something soft and delicate
As gold as Linnix fur
As feather-edged as Doozle down
As beautiful as her.
Shimma's favourite colours are
Orange, gold, magenta,
The place we've heard these can be found
Is Lowbridge garden centre.
It sounds a very special place
With plants and shrubs galore.

The perfect place to find a gift
For someone you adore.
We've heard it's near a golf course . . .
Nelly, do you know it?
Perhaps you know the plant to buy
Or even how to grow it?'

Nelly lowered her jaw to speak, and then opted for a gulp instead. Maybe she wouldn't be collecting the Nobel poetry prize at the end of the year after all. How she was going to respond to this one was anyone's guess.

She opened and closed her mouth again, and then raised her finger to draw a temporary halt to the poetic proceedings.

So the Rimes wanted to go to Lowbridge garden centre to buy a plant for Shimma's birthday. Not exactly Nelly's idea of the perfect birthday present, but then she didn't have two bumblebee heads and necks like flower stalks. The good thing was that there didn't seem to be a rhyme required in response to that. Did she know where Lowbridge garden centre was? Yes, she did, it was at the far end of the old canal road. Had she been there herself? Yes, she had, but only under sufferance. Did she know of any golden feather-edged doozle downy-type shrubs and did she know how to plant, feed and water them? No, she most certainly didn't. She didn't have a clue what Doozle down was, and as for Linnix fur? Could she explain all this in a rhyme?

No, she most certainly couldn't.

Nelly glanced over her shoulder at the garden table. Cavorta had gone indoors to get ready, leaving Shimma seated inquisitively at the garden table with both heads craned in Nelly's direction.

Nelly lowered her finger, raised her finger, lowered it and then raised it again.

Finally, and somewhat tentatively, she whispered her reply.

'Er . . . I like flowers to look at
I like flowers to sniff
I like their pretty colours
I like the way they whiff.
I'm really not an expert,

But I'm sure the place to go
Is Lowbridge garden centre
You'll love it there, I know.'

Was that a good enough reply? Nelly wasn't at all sure. But Meeta seemed happy enough with it. He seemed more than happy with it. So happy in fact that he wrapped an arm around her shoulder like a plant tendril and drew her even closer.

'Our taxi will be here soon,
We've booked it for half past,
It's so exciting, Nelly,
To leave the house at last.
We've never stepped past our front gate,
We've always stayed behind it.
The garden centre sounds divine
I hope that we can find it.'

Nelly looked across the garden. Cavorta was waiting by the back gate, and appeared to be signalling in the direction of the front driveway. Meeta relaxed his grip on Nelly's shoulder and danced rhythmically back towards the garden table.

'*Our taxi's here,*' he said with a double ruffle of Shimma's furry heads, '*it's time to go,*

Have fun while we are gone.
Show Nelly where your pyjamas are
And make sure you put them on.
Flufficate your faces
Flufficate your legs
Polish both your tippy toes
And wax your toothypegs.
Nelly will look after you,
My precious little flower!
Make sure that you behave yourself
We'll be back in an hour.'

'Gulp!' thought Nelly as the prospect of an extra half-hour's rhyming loomed. She should have guessed the Rimes meant one hour from the time they left the house! Oh well, things were going well enough. In fact, she was secretly starting to revel in the poetic challenge!

Shimma was up for it too. Up and down and all around in fact, jumping excitedly from her seat and then pirouetting like a flower faerie across the patio.

'I will be good, I will be good!
I will, I'll show you how.
I'll go and get my jim jams on
and flufficate right now.
Next week it's my birthday
I'll show you how I've grown
No one needs to help me
I can do it on my own!'

Meeta and Cavorta smiled as their daughter danced towards the house and then sprung gracefully through the open French doors.

'Keep an eye on Shimma, Nelly,
Her toothwax can get sticky,
The tiptoe polish lid is stiff
And flufficating's tricky!' said Cavorta.

Nelly glanced at the French doors, and then raised her finger one last time while she prepared her parting rhyme. To her surprise, it came to her rather quickly!

> *'Don't worry about Shimma,*
> *I'll make sure that she's OK.*
> *Now off you go, the two of you,*
> *Chop chop, be on your way!'*

With a wave of their long green arms Cavorta and Meeta finally turned the corner of the house and danced out of view in the direction of the waiting taxi.

'Heaven knows what the taxi driver will make of them!' Nelly smiled to herself. 'Mind you, you know what they say about taxi drivers, they're supposed to have seen it all!'

Nelly stood alone for a moment and drank in the atmosphere of the flower-scented garden. The perfume of the exotic flowerbeds hung like aftershave in the air.

'It's like the garden of Eden,' she swooned. 'All I need is a fig leaf . . . And an Adam. Or a Craig!'

'See you later,' she whispered to the statues,

walking towards the French doors in search of Shimma.

10

When Nelly stepped through the open French windows and entered the Rimes' home, she wasn't really sure what to expect.

She expected it to be tidy, and a bit on the posh side too. What she wasn't expecting was a flowerbed.

To Nelly's astonishment the entire floor of the Rimes' living room was carpeted with crimson flowers.

Nelly peered down at her trainers. She was ankle-deep in petals. She peered around the room. Positioned in each corner, just like the musical statues in the garden outside, silver fans were turning gently. Nelly watched mesmerized for a moment as the breeze from the fans sent waves of trembling petal heads rippling across the floor.

'I knew they liked nature,' she thought to herself, 'but there's as much garden inside the house as there is out!'

There was no obvious pathway through the flowers, and Nelly's first thought was for the impact that her soles might have on the leaves and stalks.

She pointed the toe of her trainer carefully forward and did her best to take a ballerina step across the petals.

To her relief, the flower stems and stalks weren't brittle in the slightest, springing upwards the instant she raised her foot.

Reassured that she wasn't about to leave a trail of floral destruction behind her, Nelly proceeded across the lounge to the hall.

Silver fans and a carpet of knee-high yellow flowers greeted her there, planted bulb to bulb in firm compacted floor tiles of brown peat.

Nelly nibbled her lip and tiptoed narrowly on her way.

'Are you upstairs, Shimma?
If you are, I'm coming up.
Just to make sure you're OK . . . er . . .'

Nelly paused, and then stammered. She needed a word to rhyme with 'up' . . .

'*My little buttercup!*' She smiled, reaching the end of the hallway and placing her foot on the first step of a staircase carpeted with purple petals.

Nelly eased the full weight of her front foot down on to the first step. The petals and stems of the flowers that trailed the staircase were if anything spongier underfoot than those of the hallway.

Nelly strode onwards and upwards to a landing carpeted knee-deep with starry white petals. She stood there for a moment and listened hard.

There had been no reply from Shimma the first time: perhaps she would hear her now.

'Are you in the bathroom, Shimma?
Shimma, are you there?' Nelly shouted.
'Shimma, are you up here?
If so tell me where.'

She hovered amongst the sea of white petals for a further moment and waited for a response.

It came not in the form of a rhyme, but a softly closing door.

Nelly's brow furrowed. Leafy green, with a simple lift-up wooden latch, there was nothing suspicious about the door itself, it was more the slowness with which it closed that had her wondering.

She placed the toe of her trainer down amongst the flowers that carpeted the landing, and then tiptoed as softly as she could towards the door.

The closer she came to the door, the more

aware she became of a soft droning sound issuing from within. Nelly's visit to the Ultravores came back to haunt her. Was it the buzz of an electric toothbrush or, heaven forbid, the buzz of insect wings?

She lifted the latch slowly and pushed the door wide open.

Whether the mirrored room was a bathroom or a bedroom it was difficult to say. There was no sink, no bath or shower in evidence. But the mirrors did seem to suggest bathroom.

There was no toothbrush and no insects, either winged or wingless, to behold.

There was only Shimma.

Shimma was standing in the corner of the room wearing an extremely cute pair of orange-and-cream-hooped pyjamas.

But her heads were bowed, her tiptoes were flat to the ground, and her hands were behind her back.

'*What's up Buttercup?*' asked Nelly, too concerned to waste time conjuring up a better or longer rhyme.

Shimma raised an arm slowly and pointed to the corner of the room that the open door was concealing.

'The Flufficator did it
I turned it up a touch,
But when I put my head in
it fluffed me up too much.'

Nelly peered behind the door, and then pulled back at the sight of two giant vertical brushes spinning with the speed of a car wash. The Rimes' Flufficator was like a car polisher crossed with an electric shoe brush.

'That's where the sound was coming from,' thought Nelly, reaching behind the door and switching the Flufficator off at the wall switch.

She watched as the contra spin of the giant brushes slowed to a whirr, and eventually a halt. Then she turned back to the corner of the bathroom where Shimma was standing.

Slowly, sheepishly, Shimma raised both of her heads.

'Oh dear,' thought Nelly.

One of them still resembled a bumblebee, the other had been buffed so fast it looked more like a clock dandelion.

Nelly didn't know whether to laugh or cry.

Aware that she could neither chuckle nor chortle in rhyme she decided to keep her lips zipped.

'*Look at my two faces!*' said Shimma, turning away from the mirrored wall and hopping miserably on tiptoe.

'See how fluffed one is!
The Flufficator's fluffed it
Into a ball of frizz!'

Nelly looked behind the door again. Presumably the idea of the Flufficator was to place the velvet areas of your body gently against the rotating brushes. And let the buff do its stuff so to speak.

However, Shimma's encounter with the Flufficator had taken the concept of a bad-hair day to an entirely different dimension.

Nelly smiled sympathetically and then studied her own reflection in the mirror. Thankfully for her, her own two-tone face had faded, but the embarrassment of the moment was still very much fresh in her mind. She was blowed if she was going to let Shimma suffer the way Asti had made her! Frizz? What frizz!

Nelly shuffled across the floor on her knees and placed her hands gently on Shimma's shoulders. With a bit of gentle coaxing, Shimma slowly turned away from her reflection and raised her eyes to face Nelly.

Nelly stared earnestly into each eye in turn, and allowed her lips to break. Not into a laugh or a chuckle or a snort. But a rhyme.

'*Now then little Shimma,*
What can the matter be?
I must be missing something
Cos you look just fine to me!'

It was Shimma's turn to blink now. First at Nelly, and then once more at the reflection in the wall tiles behind her.

She turned back to Nelly with confusion in her eyes.

'*Look again, you silly,*' said Shimma, pointing to each head in turn,
'*Surely you can see*
This head has gone all fluffy
It's not like it should be!'

Nelly kept a straight face, rubbed her eyes in earnest and then looked carefully at each of

Shimma's heads in turn.

> *'Shimma, don't be silly,*
> *It's your mistake, not mine*
> *There's no need to be miserable*
> *Both your heads look fine!'*

Shimma blinked again, and then turned slowly back in the direction of her reflection. She stared long and hard, patted the fluffier of her two heads with the flat of her hand, and then pirouetted slowly round to face Nelly again.

> *'Are you sure that you can't see it, Nelly?*
> *Are you sure I don't look weird?*
> *Are you sure I haven't turned my face*
> *Into a Zizzil's beard?'*

Nelly placed her hands on Shimma's shoulders again, and gave her a reassuring squeeze. She had no idea what a Zizzil was and no notion of whether the comparison between Shimma's frizzy face and a Zizzil's beard was a fair one. She just knew the answer that was needed.

'Of course I'm sure,
I'm more than sure,
I'm sure times four!
I'm . . . sure GALORE!' laughed Nelly.

The clouds passed from Shimma's eyes and a sunny sparkle returned.

'*Phew!*' she beamed. '*You've made my day!*
Let's go back outside and play.'

Nelly smiled as the natural rhythm and bounce returned to Shimma's toes.

The excitable little Rime was back to her usual self and she was right, the garden felt very much like the place to be!

Nelly rose from her knees and then dropped low again with eyebrows arched. Meeta's instructions had been quite clear before he left.

'Shimma, your dad said you must fluffícate
Your heads AND both your legs.
AND polish both your tippy toes

AND wax your toothypegs.
I see you've got your jim jams on
I see you've tried your best
To flufficate your fluffy bits
But have you done the rest?'

Shimma nodded a not entirely convincing nod. It was the kind of nod that Nelly had deployed herself on many an occasion when asked by her mum or dad if she had cleaned her teeth in the manner recommended by her dental hygeinist.

Nelly looked at her watch. The Rimes had departed fifteen minutes ago, and her rhymes were starting to come easily.

'*OK, you're done!*
Let's have some fun!' laughed Nelly.

11

Nelly let Shimma lead the way as they picked their way back through the house across the various floral carpets.

Shimma's progress was considerably more balletic than Nelly's, her pointed toes dancing across each sea of petals with the weightless ease of wings.

'How does she do that?' gasped Nelly, looking down at the clomping progress of her own trainers. She'd never felt so flat-footed.

Shimma flitted happily along the hallway and then bowed to the silver fans as she entered the lounge.

'*Petals dancing in the breeze, snowflakes softly falling,*' she sang, waving her pyjama-clad arms above her head like reeds in the wind and then leaping like a flower sprite from the French doors on to the patio.

'*The flutter of a feathered wing,*' continued Shimma,
'*Nature is my calling,*
Nature's rhythms fill my heart,
Her songs are all around.
Nature makes my spirit dance!
She lifts me off the ground!'

'Blimey,' thought Nelly, hurrying through the lounge petals just in time to see Shimma leap from the patio and spin through air like a sycamore leaf.

'There's more to Rimes than just rhymes!' she thought, jumping through the French doors and touching down with a little less grace on the patio.

Shimma beamed back at Nelly, bowed her lopsided heads and then pirouetted in the direction of the garden table.

'Excellent!' thought Nelly, with another glance at her watch. She was pretty confident now that her brain had totally mastered the art of speaking in rhyme, and was rather keen to reactivate a garden statue!

'*Do you mind if we sit?*' she asked with a smile.

'We can chat for a bit.'

'*You sit, and I'll flitter!*' said Shimma, her toes criss-crossing with the rhythm of every syllable.

'I'm a dancer, not a sitter!'

Nelly laughed and made her way across the patio to the golden table.

'*Which will it be?* . . . errrrmm . . . *Statue number three!*' she guessed, lowering herself on to the nearest available seat and peering across the lawn to see which statue her bottom would activate.

She was close, but not quite close enough, for it was the statue in the far right-hand corner of the garden that sprung to life immediately her bottom touched down.

The instant the plinth of the statue began to tinkle, Shimma pirouetted to the same corner and joined the dance.

'*Come on, Nelly, come and dance!*

Come and flitter, come and prance!' she fluted.

Nelly smiled, but declined the invitation with a wave of her hand.

'Thank you for the invite,
But I'm happy sitting here.
You dance and prance and flitter
I'll watch from here, my dear.'

Shimma flitted happily from each statue in turn,

bowing to the flowers, and dancing after the bees.

'If she keeps flitting around the garden like that all evening,' thought Nelly, 'she'll be asleep within the hour!'

Nelly lifted her wrist again, and looked confidently at her watch. Another five minutes had passed and the rhymes were coming easily to her now. Who knows, she might even write a poetry book when she got home!

She placed her hands behind her head and then leaned back to admire the pinks and reds that had begun to streak the evening sky.

'What would Mum and Dad give to live in a paradise like this?' she thought happily.

Shimma circled the flowerbed, danced past the rose trellis, pirouetted across the patio and then swooped and waved the arms of her hooped pyjamas in the direction of the garden table.

'At last she's going to sit down,' thought Nelly, secretly placing a bet with herself that statue number four would spring to life the moment Shimma's bottom was seated.

'*Can I sit on your lap instead of a seat?*' asked Shimma, springing into the air and then bending her legs into a low curtsey.

'If I sit on your lap you can tickle my feet!'

Nelly's eyes dropped to end of Shimma's legs. Tickle her feet? A monster had never asked her to do that before!

'Oh well,' she thought, placing her fingers under her seat and lifting herself away from the table so that Shimma would have room to climb on board. Feet tickling would certainly make an interesting entry in her monster sitting notebook.

The instant Nelly had resettled, Shimma sprung on to her lap.

She was lighter than Nelly expected. About as light as a large cardboard box.

'*Here's foot one!*' laughed Shimma, bending her right leg backwards like a pipe cleaner and presenting Nelly with the sole of her foot. '*Here's foot two!*' She smiled, bending the second leg impossibly backwards too.

'*Big tickles, little tickles,*

Anything will do.'

Shimma's feet were pointed just like ballerinas shoes but, close up, had the toughened appearance of polished cow horn. There were no toes to speak of, in fact given how much time she spent in the 'tiptoed' position it was possible she had worn them down to stumps.

Nelly decided to kick off with little tickles. She'd never touched the underside of a monster's foot before, and wasn't entirely sure what to expect.

She placed the tip of her index finger against the ankle end of one sole and began to work her way upwards with small spiralling movements.

Shimma's body trembled the length of her pyjamas as Nelly's fingertip probed its way towards to the stumpier end of one foot.

'*Stop wriggling,*' laughed Nelly as a ticklish tremor rippled through Shimma's arms and legs.

'*And giggling,*' Nelly added as a fluted chuckle issued from each of Shimma's furry mouths.

One by one Shimma drew her furry faces close to Nelly's cheeks.

'*Big tickles please!*' she whispered, pressing her cheeks to Nelly's like fluffy earmuffs. '*Do my ankles, then my knees!*'

Nelly chuckled.

'*Whatever you say!*' said Nelly.

'I'll tickle away!'

Nelly lifted her other arm and took firm hold of Shimma's right ankle. Then with a mischievous chuckle she ran her finger firmly across the underside of Shimma's foot. Shimma's bottom slid across Nelly's lap, and her arms flapped upwards into the air as the bigger tickle prodded home.

'*My ankles, Nelly! And my knees!*' she hooted.

'Then all over, Nelly, please!'

Nelly puffed out her cheeks and then went for it big time. In a matter of seconds she had Shimma wriggling like a worm on a hot plate.

'*Now my elbows! And my legs!*' said Shimma.

'*Don't forget my toothypegs!*'

Nelly caught her breath. Ticklish teeth? How weird was that?

With an affectionate ruffle of Shimma's

frizziest head, Nelly ran her hands up and down Shimma's body like a concert pianist sitting at a grand piano.

Shimma's hooped pyjamas folded into a heap of uncontrollable giggles.

'I'd have passed out by now,' thought Nelly, returning her fingers for an encore and then running her fingernails delicately across the green enamel of Shimma's teeth.

The lips of Shimma's frizzier head opened wide with ecstatic pleasure, as the tip of Nelly's fingernail danced across her gums.

'*Don't forget these teeth as well,*

they really tickle, can't you tell!' said Shimma, swinging her un-flufficated face directly in front of Nelly's and opening her velvet mouth wide.

Nelly grimaced, raised her other hand and tickled both sets of gnashers at once. With every scrape of her finger, a soft waxy coating was sliding from Shimma's enamel and collecting under her nails.

'*Tickle time is over now!*' laughed Nelly, wiping

her fingertips on the arms of the garden chair.

'*No more, I insist.*

'I've tickled every part of you, there can't be one I've missed.

My monster sitting service always aims to please.

But all your wiggle jiggling is nobbling my knees!'

Shimma's faces broke out into two appreciative but slightly disappointed smiles. She'd have been happy to wiggle and jiggle all evening.

She swung her necks back into a V position, and smiled back at Nelly from two sides.

'I've got an idea, Nelly!
Why don't I tickle you!
Tell me where you like it best
And I'll make you jiggle too!'

Nelly leaned back in her chair and squirmed. She hated being tickled. She loathed being tickled. She would rather eat the carpet in the lounge than be tickled.

'*There's nowhere that I like it!*
Tickles aren't for me.
My funny bones can't take it
So you just leave me be!'

A broad smile broke across Shimma's frizzy face, while a puzzled look broke across the other.

'*Everyone like tickles, Nelly!*' said Shimma, raising her hooped arms and flexing her biceps like a muscleman.

'*Tickles make you strong!*
Maybe you're not ticklish
Maybe that's what's wrong?'

'*I wish I wasn't ticklish,*' laughed Nelly.
'Just like my sister Asti.
She missed out on the funny bones.
All her bones are nasty.'

Shimma lowered her arms and swung both of her heads directly in front of Nelly's face.

'A sister, Nelly, a sister?
You should have said before
I'd love to have a sister
Please please tell me more!!'

Nelly sighed. Just when things were going so well, she was being asked to talk about the Devil's spawn herself.

A conversation about Asti really didn't belong in a garden as beautiful as this, on an evening as wonderful as this.

Nelly stared into Shimma's eyes. Both frizzy and velvet faces were equally imploring.

'OK, little Shimma,
If you really want to know
I'll tell you all about her.
Ready . . . ?'

Shimma nodded.

'Here I go . . .
My sister's name's Astilbe,
Asti is for short.

From the day that we were born
The two of us have fought.
The pair of us are twins, that means
We were born on the same day.
We could have shared a special bond
But we went the other way
The two of us are poles apart.
The stuff she likes, I don't.
All the things she says she'll do
Are all the things I won't.
She has no time for monsters.
She thinks that you're all strange.
She's always been the way she is,
She's never going to change.
She calls me names, she winds me up
She can be quite a bitch.
If you put her in a fairy tale,
She'd have to be the witch.'

Shimma tilted merrily from side to side with the rhythm of Nelly's verse, and then raised her arm above her head to interject.

'If I got my own sister
Or a brother came along
I'd want them to be nice to me
Cos being nasty's wrong.'

Nelly smiled.

'Don't worry about Asti.
Asti's got diarrhoea.
She brought it on herself, you know!
. . .
. . .
. . .'

Nelly frowned . . .

Shimma danced from side to side.

Nelly thought . . .

Shimma shifted from side to side again, and urged Nelly to continue.

Nelly faltered . . .

Shimma swung her faces close up to Nelly's and implored her to complete the rhyme.

Nelly swallowed hard, and then started

to sweat . . .

Shimma's shoulders began to slacken, and her necks began to wilt.

Nelly's heart beat began to batter the inside of her ribcage. She rung her brain out like tea towel, but it was no use.

She couldn't think of a word that rhymed with diarrhoea!

12

Shimma's lifeless body lay cradled in Nelly's arms. It was one minute past seven. Just one minute past the hour that Nelly had originally expected the Rimes to return home. She had lasted the full hour that she had expected to have to last, but the Rimes had changed the schedule! She had done so well. She had rhymed everything so beautifully. And now what?

Nelly's brain jackhammered.

Birea?
Cirea?
Firea?
Girea?
Hirea?
Jirea?
Kirea?

There must be a word that rhymed with diarrhoea. There just had to be!

Lirea?
Mirea?
Nirea?
Pirea?
Quirea?

It was hopeless.

'Oh, shut up, will you!' snapped Nelly, finally losing patience with the musical statue that was pirouetting and tinkling rhythmically in the corner of the Rimes' garden. 'Can't you see I'm trying to THINK!'

She lifted her bottom from her garden seat, and stopped the statue dead.

Rirea?
Sirea?
Tirea?
Uirea?
Virea?

Nelly slid her left arm up and past Shimma's shoulders. She needed to check if her eyelids were still flickering, but her necks had wilted like flower stalks and her heads were dangling lifelessly just inches from the ground.

Nelly needed a rhyme and she needed it FAST!

Her memory scoured the pages of the poetry books she had been reading at school. But it was no good. Diarrhoea just wasn't a subject that any of the classical poets had ever touched upon. Wordsworth, Keats, Byron, the whole floppy-cuffed lot of them were no good to Nelly now.

She had already reached the hopeless end of the alphabet, but decided out of pure desperation to interrogate the final few possibilities.

Wirea?
Xirea?
Yirea?
Zirea?

It was worth a try, but pointless.

Nelly carried Shimma over to an area of the

lawn that was bathed in evening light, and gently lowered her on to the grass. There was no movement in the little Rime's body at all, no wiggle, no jiggle, no dance; all of her exuberance, all of her buzz had simply drained away.

Nelly lifted each of Shimma's heads in turn and gently straightened her necks into the V shape they were meant to be. Lowering her ear to Shimma's chest, she listened through the hoops of her pyjamas for a heart beat. She lowered her ear further down to Shimma's waistline and fancied, just half fancied that she could hear one.

'I'll ring someone!' she thought. 'I'll ring my dad! He does crosswords and everything!'

She thrust her hand into the pocket of her jeans and stabbed the key pads of her phone.

After five infuriating rings, her dad picked up the phone.

'Dad, do you know any words that rhyme with diarrhoea?' gushed Nelly.

'I beg your pardon!' asked her dad, more than a little confused.

'I need a word that rhymes with DIARRHOEA!'

shouted Nelly. 'If you don't know one, ask Mum, and if she doesn't know one, look in the dictionary!'

Nelly's dad fell silent for a moment.

'IT'S AN EMERGENCY!' said Nelly. 'ASK EVERYONE!'

'But—' stammered her dad.

'Ring me back!' said Nelly, cutting him off and raising the phone to make her next call.

'I'll ring Grit,' she gasped. 'Maybe there's a Huffaluk word that rhymes with diarrhoea!'

Grit answered the phone after only three rings, but there were no Huffaluk words that could help her.

'I'll ring Lump!' she panted. 'Maybe there's a Dendrileg word that rhymes with diarrhoea!'

But it took just one ring to inform her that there wasn't.

Nelly paced anxiously across the lawn to the patio, and then stared at her watch. It was eight minutes past seven now. There were still twenty-two rhymeless minutes to go before Meeta and Cavorta were due home!

Nelly raced back to Shimma and dropped down by her side. Parting the frizz that had been fluffed up by the Flufficator, she leaned forward and blew gently on to the eyelid.

There was movement. It was almost imperceptible. But there was movement!

Nelly rocketed the alphabet through her head again, in a desperate search for a rhyme, and then reversed backwards from the letter Z to A.

It was hopeless. She had no words, her dad had no words, Grit had no words, Lump had no words. What if Meeta and Cavorta had no words! What would happen to Shimma then?

Nelly's fist tightened around her mobile, and the alphabet jumbled and tumbled through her brain once again. She added letters, subtracted letters, contorted letters, pleaded with letters, but the rhyme she needed was nowhere to be found.

'I'll ring every monster I know,' she said, raising her index finger to open her address book and then jumping as her ringtone heralded an incoming call.

It was her dad.

'Have you got one?' squeaked Nelly desperately.

'No,' came the killer reply.

'KEEP THINKING!' squealed Nelly, cutting her dad off after one word, and making a desperate call to the Muggots.

'Hell—'

'It's Nelly,' interrupted Nelly. 'Do you know any words that rhyme with diarrhoea?'

'What's diarrhoea?' asked Leafmould, a little puzzled by the nature of Nelly's enquiry.

'Don't ask!' said Nelly. 'This is really important!' she stressed. 'Do you, or Agar or anyone you know, know a Muggot word that rhymes with DIARRHOEA?'

There was a pause. Too long a pause for Nelly's liking.

'CALL ME BACK!' she gasped, cutting Leafmould off and making a call to the Pipplewaks.

But whichever monster she rang, the answer was the same. Neither the Pipplewaks, the Cowcumbers, the Altigators, the Thermitts, the Ultravores, the Water Greeps, the Squurms, the Grerks nor the Polarbores had a word that even remotely rhymed with diarrhoea. Everyone was desperately keen to help, and every monster to a tentacle said they would scour their dictionaries at home for an answer. But no answer proved forthcoming!

Nelly stared miserably across the lawn at Shimma's lifeless body. Meeta and Cavorta would be back shortly. How would they ever forgive her!

She was clean out of ideas, clean out of numbers to ring, and even lower on credits. It was hopeless. If only she hadn't said that she would monster sit. If only she had stayed at home.

13

Nelly rested Shimma's heads in her lap and stroked the cheeks of each velvet face in turn. The glimmer of life that she had seen earlier had all but vanished now.

Nelly lifted her eyes and gazed around the garden. There was movement all around her, in the buzz of the bees, the flap of a bird's wing, the rustle of the leaves, the passing of the clouds: everywhere she looked there were painful reminders of the life force that Shimma so keenly celebrated.

Nelly closed her eyes and thought hard again. She had wrung her brain cells dry with desperation but it was no good.

She was no good.

Nobel prize for poetry? She had more chance of winning the marathon in flip-flops.

'It's your fault, Asti,' she groaned. 'If you hadn't given yourself diarrhoea, I wouldn't have said the word in the first place. Cry for help? You'll be crying for help when I've finished with you.'

Nelly levered herself back on to her elbows and then slumped backwards with her shoulder blades flat to the lawn.

'I hate her!' she scowled, her eyes reddening like the sky. 'I detest her. I loathe her. I . . . hate her,' she sighed, running out of transitive verbs.

For the next ten minutes Nelly sat in mournful silence, with Shimma cradled in her arms.

Ayrea, blirea, chirea, flirea, xjzirea? All the permutations she could think of produced nothing but a pain in her temples.

Her mind had become a word jam. A useless rhymeless word jam.

Nelly leaned forward and blew gently on to each of Shimma's eyelids in turn.

'Yes!' gasped Nelly with relief, as the faintest of flickers registered at the centre of the frizz. 'There's still hope!' she thought, darting her eyes to the back gate at the sound of tyres on gravel.

'They're home!' she gasped, lowering Shimma to the lawn and springing to her feet. 'How am I going to tell them? What am I going to say?'

Nelly's mind jammed even more. Whatever explanation she came up with she was going to have to deliver it IN RHYME! Otherwise Meeta and Cavorta might end up flat out on the lawn as well!

Nelly froze with indecision.

She could hear taxi doors opening and closing now, and the sound of footsteps on gravel. They were approaching the back gate!

A lump the size of a toffee apple formed in Nelly's throat. She could see Meeta now. He was waving to her from behind the gate.

Nelly swallowed hard and then harder still. The toffee apple wouldn't dislodge.

She sighed heavily and waited for Meeta to enter the garden. But, quite unexpectedly, he didn't. Instead he ducked behind the rose trellis and waved again. Not so much a greeting wave, more a beckoning wave.

Nelly stared back blankly.

Cavorta's two heads had appeared now. Her velvet mouths were smiling broadly and her hands were beckoning excitedly too.

'Oh, no, they want to show me what they've bought at the garden centre,' groaned Nelly. 'Oh, my God,' she whispered. 'It's Shimma's birthday next week. What kind of birthday will it be now?'

Nelly waved weakly back in the direction of the back gate, and then looked across the lawn to where Shimma was lying out of view.

'How on earth am I going to explain?' Nelly groaned. And in rhyme in RHYME in **RHYME!**

Sadly, dejectedly, guiltily, Nelly made her way across the garden towards the back gate.

'They're going to kill me when they find out what's happened,' she whimpered. 'It's all Ast's fault. I could kill her!'

Meeta and Cavorta were in no mood to kill anyone. They were beside themselves with excitement.

Before Nelly could even begin to break the news, they drew her through the open gate with a flurry of eyebrows and waves.

'Nelly, it's been brilliant,
We loved the garden centre!
The colours were just wonderful,
Orange, gold, magenta!
We found the perfect present
For Shimma, can you guess?
We don't want her to see it, look!
Spirea, Golden Princess!'

Nelly stared grimly at the large green flower pot that Meeta was concealing behind the rose trellis. Her eyes drifted sadly from leaf to leaf and flower to flower, and then fixed for a moment on the plant label.

Did Meeta just say what she thought he'd just said?

Cavorta ran her fingers delicately across the delicate golden flowers of the birthday shrub and whispered excitedly.

'Behold our birthday secret!

Shimma's going to love it.
No flower in our garden
Will ever rise above it.'

Nelly nodded slowly and then stepped forward to examine the label. Meeta and Cavorta beamed excitedly as Nelly's eyes saucered open.

'*Great! Wait!*' she shouted, snatching the tub from Meeta's arms and racing through the back gate.

Meeta and Cavorta danced up and down on the spot and then watched with open-mouthed horror as their beloved daughter's birthday surprise disappeared across the lawn.

'*DON'T WORRY ABOUT ASTI!*' shouted Nelly.
'*ASTI'S GOT DIARRHOEA*
SHE BROUGHT IT ON HERSELF, YOU KNOW.
LOOK! THIS PLANT'S CALLED SPIREA!'

Nelly dropped to her knees beside Shimma, and dumped the surprise birthday shrub on the lawn beside her.

Meeta and Cavorta stopped dancing, and tumbled through the garden gate in pursuit.

Nelly's heart leaped and her spirits soared, as one by one Shimma's eyelids were beginning to flicker.

'It's working!' thought Nelly, careful not to speak out loud for fear of returning Shimma to a rhymeless coma. 'Spirea rhymes with diarrhoea! Who'd have thought it! Thank you, thank you, thank you, Lowbridge garden centre!'

Shimma's eyes opened and then blinked groggily. The flexibility had come back in her neck, and the strength was returning to her legs.

'*Look at your face!*' gasped Meeta, pirouetting across the lawn, and then prancing in front of the flower pot to conceal the birthday shrub. '*It's all over the place!*'

Shimma turned her two faces towards Nelly and frowned.

'*Ooh, you big fibber, Nelly,*
I might be feeling dizzy
But I knew the Fluffìcator had
Made my face look frizzy!'

Nelly shrugged her shoulders. As far as she was concerned, a frizzy face had been the least of Shimma's problems.

'*Hello, Shimma darling,*' said Cavorta, looping one of her necks through the air to check that her daughter's other face was OK.

'*Were you having a little sleep?*
We thought that you'd be having fun
Not lying in a heap!'

Shimma patted the cheeks of her face and then sat up.

'*Something happened earlier,*
I'm trying to think back.
One minute we were talking,
The next thing it went black!'

Meeta and Cavorta looked from the plant pot to Shimma, and then from Shimma to Nelly. They were as confused as their daughter.

Nelly smiled sweetly at the three of them and

then pressed her index finger tightly to her lips. As far as she was concerned, she had said all she was going to say that evening and had rhymed all she was going to rhyme.

As Meeta dropped discreetly to his knees to hide the plant pot behind his back, Nelly jumped to her feet.

A second crunch of driveway gravel had announced the arrival of her dad.

Nelly wasted no time in making her escape. She shook Meeta by the hand, blew kisses to Cavorta and Shimma, and hurried silently across the lawn in the direction of the back gate.

Meeta and Shimma watched in velvet-faced astonishment as Nelly vanished from their garden without so much as a word or a rhyme.

Down the drive she ran, wrenching opened the passenger door of the Maestro and waving her dad off the drive.

'Sorry I was late,' said her dad, reversing the car carefully on to Barleysugar Drive. 'Did you find the rhyme you needed?'

Nelly nodded, but kept her lips firmly shut.

'We couldn't think of one for the life of us,' said Nelly's dad, indicating right as he approached the Pontefract roundabout. 'There *are* no words that rhyme with diarrhoea, as far as I know!'

Nelly kept her lips zipped.

'I'll tell you another word that can't be rhymed too,' said Nelly's dad, who after scouring the dictionary had become a bit of an expert on the subject. 'LEMON!' he said, with a tap of the steering wheel. 'Nothing rhymes with lemon! Who'd have thought it, eh! Mind you, tangerine sounds a bit of a toughie too!' he laughed.

Nelly remained silent and slumped wearily down in her seat.

In fact they were a full mile further down the road before she permitted her lips to part.

'I'm going to kill Asti!' she growled.

THE WATT WATTS
At No. 56

1

It was Frosties for breakfast the next morning. A very frosty Nelly and an extremely frosty Asti sat in silence at the breakfast table exchanging the iciest of glares.

'You nearly killed her, you moron,' said Nelly, finally breaking the ice with a crunch of cold toast.

'I NEARLY KILLED HER?' snapped Asti. 'You're the one that said diarrhoea!'

'You're the one that GOT diarrhoea in the first place!' snarled Nelly. 'I wouldn't have said diarrhoea if you hadn't given yourself diarrhoea in the first place with your pathetic cry for help!'

'Excuse me!' said Asti, removing one of her mum's hairs from her crispbread. 'What gives you the right to talk about me or my diarrhoea to monsters anyway? Mum! Tell Nelly not to talk about me to monsters. I don't want them knowing the slightest thing about me.'

'Don't flatter yourself, there isn't much to know,' said Nelly, lifting a mug of cold tea to her lips and gulping. 'Apart from the fact that you're a squit bot.'

The girls' mum tightened the cord on her dressing gown and carried her coffee through to the lounge.

'I don't want to know!' she growled. 'If you two girls can't talk to each other nicely, then don't talk to each other at all.'

'But she's talking to monsters about me!' protested Asti. 'She's telling ugly, slimy, hundred-headed monsters all about me. I'm private property, I'm not just there to be talked about. Tell her not to talk to monsters about me!'

It was customary on occasions like this for Mum to call upon her husband to mediate between the two warring factions. But, much to Mum's annoyance, Clifford T. Morton had forecast a bitter frost the evening before, and had left for work early that morning, to escape being bitten.

Nelly's mum closed the door of the lounge behind her and left the two girls to argue.

'Slug face,' hissed Asti.

'Lentil brain,' snapped Nelly.

'Plague person,' hissed Asti.

'No boyfriend,' said Nelly, chopping her sister off at the school socks with the cruellest insult of all.

Asti's lips froze in mid-munch. Her eyes darkened and her knuckles whitened.

'Oops!' thought Nelly, glancing across the table over the top of her mug. 'I said the wrong thing there.'

'I WOULD HAVE A BOYFRIEND,' screamed Asti, thumping her plate with her fist, and detonating an explosion of crispbread crumbs high up into the air. 'IF IT WASN'T FOR YOU. YOU'RE THE ONE THAT TURNED DARREN AGAINST ME. YOU AND YOUR SCUMMY MONSTER FRIENDS HAVE TURNED EVERYONE AGAINST ME!'

Nelly kept her mug raised, in case anything bigger than a crispbread crumb suddenly grenaded her way.

'RUBBISH!' Nelly glared. 'THAT'S ABSOLUTE RUBBISH AND YOU KNOW IT. THE REASON EVERYONE IS HORRIBLE TO YOU IS BECAUSE YOU'RE SO HORRIBLE TO

ME. SO WHAT IF I HAD AN ACCIDENT AT THE ULTRAVORES', SO WHAT IF MY FACE LOOKED A BIT WEIRD, SO WHAT IF I LIKE GOING MONSTER SITTING AND SO WHAT IF I DON'T WEAR MAKE-UP! AND SO WHAT IF I DON'T EAT CRISPBREADS! YOU'RE THE ONE WITH THE PROBLEM NOT ME!' shouted Nelly, lowering her mug regardless.

Asti scanned the breakfast bar for something to plunge into her sister's heart, but decided a teaspoon wouldn't be quite up to the job.

'WELL, YOU'RE THE ONE WITH NO FASHION SENSE!' she screeched, lurching from her breakfast stool and plunging her breakfast plate into the sink.

'And you're the one with no boyfriend,' smirked Nelly, closing her teeth triumphantly around her final piece of toast.

Asti's shoulders lurched forward and her eyes darkened like olives.

'You're so dead!' she growled resisting the temptation to pull a bread knife from the knife block. 'You are so SO dead!' she fumed, wheeling round empty-handed and stomping back upstairs to develop her murderous thoughts further.

'AND YOU'RE SO SO SINGLE!' laughed Nelly, slipping from her stool and placing her own breakfast plate calmly into the suds.

As the plate slipped beneath the suds to the bottom of the bowl, the smirk on Nelly's face slid simultaneously from view

She reached for the dishcloth and sighed. She hated arguing with her sister. What was the point of it? Why couldn't they ever get on? Surely other twins weren't like this? Surely two sisters of the same age could actually live in peace together?

She lifted each of the breakfast plates in turn and watched ruefully as the suds slid like tears on to the drainer.

She couldn't help feeling a bit guilty. She had hurt Asti this time. Really hurt her. Name calling was one thing but the area of boyfriends was much too sensitive for Asti to cope with. There were many important issues in the world. There was global warming.

There were carbon footprints. There was war

in the Middle East. There was famine in the Third World.

For Asti, there was just Boyfriends.

'It's still her fault,' thought Nelly, replaying the events of Monday through her mind. 'She made fun of me at school, she made fun of me at the disco. She gave herself diarrhoea, knowing full well there are next to no words that rhyme with it. She always ALWAYS starts it.

'Trouble is,' she thought, 'I'm far too good at finishing it.'

Despite all the justification she had for squaring up with her sister, the double rapier-plunge about Asti's lack of a boyfriend had left Nelly feeling more than a little bit sheepish. With any argument between two people there are places one should never go. Nelly had been there twice, in the space of one breakfast.

'Maybe I should apologize,' thought Nelly, pulling the plug from the bowl and dumping it on the drainer. 'Maybe I should tell her that Darren Leadbetter fancies her?' she thought, as she watched the suds spiral down the plughole.

The final swirled eddied down the plughole with a gurgle.

'The hell I will,' she growled.

2

Two more gurgles greeted Nelly when she returned upstairs to her bedroom. One came from the plughole in the bathroom, courtesy of Asti emptying the sink, the second and slightly gurglier gurgle came from the end of Nelly's monster sitting phone.

'Hello?' said Nelly, dropping her school shoes beside her bed and answering the phone before it had barely had time to complete its first trilling ring. It was unusual to receive a call from a monster so early in the morning.

She sat on the edge of her bed and listened intently as the gurgle was followed by a bang.

'Slimy,' she thought, hazarding a guess at the mystery monster's appearance. 'No, scaly,' she thought, as it delivered its first words.

'Please excuse me, Nelly, what what!' crackled

the voice, 'I wasn't expecting you to answer the phone, so quickly, Nelly. I had a mouthful of Leru milk! Terribly bad manners, what what!'

Nelly pointed her toes in the direction of her school shoes, but kept her attention very much on the caller. She hadn't heard a monster's voice quite like this before.

'That's OK!' she smiled, changing her mind about scaly and opting for spiky instead. 'Would you like me to come and monster sit for you?'

'Yes yes, what what!' crackled the voice. 'Would you do that, Nelly? We'd be ever so grateful if you could. What what!'

'What's with all the what whats?' thought Nelly, sticking her tongue out as her sister stampeded past her bedroom door.

Nelly glanced at her watch. She had to be leaving for school in eight minutes. Her shoes weren't on. Her teeth weren't cleaned, her face wasn't washed and her scrunchy wasn't scrunched.

She had a choice, either ask the monster to call back later (which seemed a bit rude) or get all the monster sitting details she needed as quickly as she could. (Which seemed a bit rude. But maybe she could do it without appearing rude.)

'We've heard all about you, Nelly,' the monster continued with a crackle and a hum. 'Very impressed with what we hear. What what!'

'When would you like me to monster sit?' asked Nelly, wiggling her feet into her school shoes, and reaching across to her desk, to grab her diary and her pen. She had decided to take as direct an approach as possible.

The monster continued with a hum and then an excited crackle. 'Saturday afternoon. Two till five if you could.'

Nelly flipped open her monster sitting diary and confirmed what she already suspected.

'Yes, I'm free all day Saturday.' She reached over into her drawer for her strawberry gel pen. 'Two till five will be fine. Is there anything special you'd like me to bring?'

'Nothing really,' crackled the monster, 'apart from rubber gloves.'

The toe of Nelly's school shoe skewed across the carpet. 'Rubber gloves?' she thought.

'Rubber gloves must mean slimy.'

'Two till five it is then,' she said with a smile, scribbling the appointment hurriedly into her diary, and then glancing at her watch again. 'Goodbye!' she said, standing up from her bed and scouring her room for a scrunchy.

'Don't you need our name and address?' crackled the monster, interjecting before Nelly had time to put the phone down. 'Perhaps you need our phone number too!'

Nelly sat back down on the bed, pressed the receiver to her ear again and brought herself to her senses. What was she thinking of?

'I'm so sorry,' she blustered. 'It's just that I need to be leaving for school very soon. Please do tell me your name and address. We wouldn't get very far without those!'

Nelly's apology was warmly accepted and details were exchanged.

'Is that WHACK with a c and a k?' Nelly asked, shaking her strawberry gel pen aggressively to coax some ink into the nib.

'W . . . A . . . K,' replied the monster. 'My name

is Wak, what what! My wife's name is Zap, and we have three children, Volta, Fusea and Urth.'

Wak paused to allow Nelly time to write down his family's names and then furnished Nelly with their telephone number and then their address.

'We live at Number 56 Jamboree Grove, what what!'

Nelly jumped. The front door of the house had just closed with a slam. That meant Asti had already left for school. She looked at her watch and groaned again. She was going to be late for sure.

'Oh well,' she thought. There was only one more question to ask, so she may as well ask it.

'And what kind of monsters are you?' she asked politely.

'We're Wattwatts, what what!' crackled the voice.

'That figures,' thought Nelly.

'So that's Saturday, two till five, Number 56 Jamboree Grove,' murmured Nelly, reading the appointment back to herself to make sure she hadn't scribbled it down too fast.

'Look forward to seeing you Saturday, Nelly,

what what!' crackled the monster.

'I look forward to meeting you too!' replied Nelly, although the only thing she wanted to acquaint herself with at the moment was a toothbrush. 'See you Saturday!' she said, replacing the phone abruptly and racing into the bathroom.

'Three monsters in one week!' she smiled, spitting a mouthful of fluoride into the sink. 'That's a record!'

3

Nelly's journey to school that morning began as a fast-paced walk, stepped up to a trot and then exploded into a full-blown gallop. She hated being late for anyone or anything. Even school.

Living just seven short streets from school had its advantages and disadvantages. The clear advantage was that both Nelly and her sister could leave home late and still arrive on time. The disadvantage was that leaving home any later than late left little or no time to make up. Hence the gallop.

Nelly sprinted around the corner of Sweet Street and into the top end of Candy Close. To her dismay there were no other stragglers in sight.

Nelly raised her watch to her face and groaned. No wonder. It was two minutes past nine! She wasn't just late. She was heading for a detention.

She slapped her arm around her school bag and put on a spurt that propelled her down the street like an Olympic sprinter.

Had someone had a stopwatch handy she might even have broken the land speed record for one hundred metres in regulation school shoes, except, for no apparent reason, she suddenly and unexpectedly pulled up.

The soles of her shoes crunched down hard on to the pavement on the approach to Dolly Way. Her grip loosened on her school bag, and her shoulders sagged.

Had she pulled a hamstring? No. Had she snapped her Achilles tendon? No. Had she forgotten to pack her lunch box? No. It was far worse than that.

'I said I'd walk into town with Craig on Saturday afternoon!' she gasped. 'Now I've arranged to go to the Wattwatts!'

She'd forgotten. She'd completely forgotten their first date! And now she was double booked!

Nelly's cheeks reddened with the puff of the run, and the embarrassment of having to let either Craig or the Wattwatts down. Thoughts of being late for school and the prospect of her second ever detention seemed of piffling importance now.

'It's all Asti's fault,' she panted, not entirely sure why, but still angry enough with her sister to lump her with the blame.

She couldn't cancel Craig. It was going to be their first proper date! She couldn't cancel the Wattwatts. She had NEVER EVER let a monster family down before. How she was going to resolve this little mess was anyone's guess.

Nelly looked at her watch and sighed. It was five past nine. The school register would be over, and morning assembly would have begun.

But school was the last thing on her mind now.

'What am I going to do?' she sighed, dropping her school bag to the floor and dragging it slowly behind her. 'What will Craig think? What will Wak think?' She trudged despondently into Brittle Street.

Her first glimpse of the school confirmed her worst fears. The school gates were shut. Unless

she scaled the fence, entry could only be gained by a press of the '*Hello, it's a very late Nelly Morton here, please can I have a detention, Mr Sturgiss*' entry-phone button.

Nelly cut across Dolly Way and stopped at the school perimeter fence.

'I know!' she thought, her face brightening in spite of the impending detention. 'Craig can come with me! He said he thought monster sitting was cool! He even said he'd like to go monster sitting with me. Well, maybe he can!'

Nelly lifted her finger to the school entry-phone buzzer and pressed it excitedly. It was a big call. Nelly had never taken a friend monster sitting before, apart from her sister Asti, and Asti hardly qualified as a friend.

Nelly hovered by the school gates and waited for the entry phone to respond.

'The minute I get home this evening, I'll ring the Wattwatts to ask them if it's OK!'

'Hellooo,' droned a voice from the school office that had all the charisma of a paperclip.

Nelly pressed her mouth to the grille of the entry phone and handed herself in.

'It's Nelly the Monster Sit . . . I mean Nelly Morton,' said Nelly. 'Class 8c. I'm late,' she added, deciding to come clean.

'Please come to the office,' droned the paperclip.

'With pleasure!' smiled Nelly.

4

One hour's detention was Nelly's punishment for being late. Scheduled for Friday after school.

'Cool,' said Craig, toe-poking another stone across the playground at morning break time.

'Really?' said Nelly.

'Really,' said Craig.

Nelly ran the equation through her mind. How getting a detention made her cool, she wasn't exactly sure, especially as it meant an extra hour longer in school. Still, if it was cool with Craig, then maybe she'd work on being late for school again.

Actually on second thoughts, maybe she'd just recommend it to Asti. Her sister could do with upping her cool credits, plus the more time she spent in detention the less time Nelly would have to deal with her at home.

'How were the Rimes?' asked Craig, sliding the back of his school blazer down the sports hall wall, and parking his bum on the grass.

'Don't ask!' puffed Nelly, looking round suddenly and wondering where he'd gone.

Craig plucked a blade of grass from the turf and began to shred it with his fingers.

'No, DO ask!' said Nelly, looking down and dumping her school bag on the grass beside him. 'I'm just saying don't ask because it was nearly a disaster!'

Craig waited for Nelly to settle on to her makeshift pillow, and then smiled. 'Poetry let you down, did it?'

Nelly bridled at the thought and shook her head. 'No, it didn't! I was doing really well for fifty-six minutes! It was my moron of a sister who let me down.'

'Did she go with you?' asked Craig. 'I thought you weren't talking to each other!'

'We're not!' said Nelly, plucking her own blade of grass from the lawn and then launching into a rhyme by rhyme account of her visit to the Rimes.

'Beef stock cubes and what?' grimaced Craig, standing up at the sound of the break-time bell.

Nelly looked at her watch and sighed. She had been so busy talking about the Rimes she hadn't even mentioned the Wattwatts. Would Craig want to come with her to Jamboree Grove on Saturday? That particular conversation would have to wait until lunchtime break.

'Instant Whip and lemon juice,' she squirmed. 'It was a cry for help apparently.'

'That's hilarious!' laughed Craig, hooking his bag over his shoulder, and then pulling Nelly up from the turf with his hand.

'Trying to think of a word to rhyme with diarrhoea isn't hilarious,' protested Nelly. 'It's nigh on impossible!'

'You should have said *runs* instead,' said Craig. 'There are stacks of words that rhyme with *runs* . . . guns, buns, suns . . .'

'Yes, all right!' said Nelly. 'All right, clever clogs, I never thought of it at the time!'

'Nuns,' said Craig, releasing Nelly's hand at

the sight of the headmaster.

'Puns,' said Nelly, brushing the dirt from her school bag. 'Tons,' she added, not wanting to be out-rhymed by a novice.

'Stuns!' added Craig, pointing himself in the direction of the science lab.

Nelly pointed herself in the direction of the art department and faltered. She couldn't let Craig have the last rhyme.

. . .

. . .

'Juns,' she said with a wave.

'JUNS?' shouted Craig. 'What's a Jun when it's at home?'

'It's a monster word,' said Nelly mischievously. 'It means meet me here again at lunchtime, I want to ask you something!'

Craig raised his arm and then scooted across the playground to catch up with Darren Leadbetter and the rest of his mates.

Nelly ran in the other direction and joined the crowds of other pupils trying to file through the entrance of the art building all at the same time.

'I hope Craig doesn't tell Darren about Asti's squits,' she thought, with a nibble of her lip. 'Asti will kill me if he does.'

5

Craig didn't tell Darren.

He told Darren, Colin, Josh and three of his other mates too.

By lunchtime, Asti's bowel movements were the talk of Year 8.

She first got wind of it as she stepped out of geography, the very first lesson after morning break.

'Was that an earthquake?' said Colin Lampton in a loud voice. 'Asti, did you feel that? I'm sure I heard a loud rumble!'

Asti looked up from her timetable to find Darren Leadbetter and his mates grinning at her from the bottom of the stairwell.

She got wind of it a second time as she came out of chemistry, the final lesson before lunch.

'Mmmm, time for lunch,' said Josh Waites, as

the class filed out of the classroom. 'I wonder what's for dinner. I hope it's Instant Whip, beef stock cubes and lemon juice,' he said, licking his lips like a giraffe.

She third got wind of it when Natalie Dupré scurried up to her in the dinner queue and tugged her arm. 'Everyone knows you've got the squits!' she whispered. 'Nelly must have told them!'

Asti turned whiter than a cue ball and gripped Natalie's arm. 'I have NOT got the squits!' she hissed. 'I HAD the squits, but I have NOT got them now!'

Natalie's knees buckled as Asti's fingers sunk through the arm of her uniform, stopping all blood circulation right down to the bone. 'Is anyone looking at me?' Asti hissed again. 'Have a look behind us. Is anyone looking at me?'

Natalie scanned the dinner queue and then gulped. 'Everyone!' she squeaked.

Asti looked over her shoulder to find a long file of grinning faces leering at her with torment-filled eyes.

'Help,' squeaked Colin Lampton from the back of the queue.

'Was that a cry for help?' shouted Josh Waites, cupping his hand to his ear.

'Help!' came another squeak from the middle of the queue.

'There it is again!' laughed Colin, peering down the line. 'It definitely sounded like a cry for help!'

'Help!' came the third squeak.

'Help,' came a fourth.

Asti's face fizzed crimson with embarrassment. Natalie was right. Nelly must have told everyone. Not anyone. EVERYONE! INCLUDING DARREN LEADBETTER.

If she could have taken a cyanide pill right there and then, she would have done.

She didn't have long to wait for the first raspberry. She had even less time to wait for the next. Before she knew it, the entire dinner queue had broken into a chorus of squit impressions and 'Helps!'

With her dignity in tatters, Asti burst from the queue.

Everyone in the dinner queue sniggered and stared as she thundered down the corridor in the direction of the main playground. Pupils arriving late for dinner sidestepped, dodged and reeled as she barged her way through and past them. Asti was on the warpath. And one pupil in the school who hadn't see her coming was Nelly.

Nelly was sitting on her school bag with her back to the sports hall wall, waiting for Craig to join her. Rather than take her sandwich box into the assembly hall, she had smuggled it outside to share with Craig.

She had just prised the lid off the Tupperware and was about to break her banana into two halves when she was dragged to her knees by her ponytail.

'HOW COULD YOU?' screamed Asti, tightening her grip around Nelly's hair and then wrenching upwards, fast and hard.

Nelly squealed with pain and dropped her banana into the dirt. 'LET GO!' she screamed, paddling across the grass on her hand and knees and then, finally, managing to stagger to her feet.

Asti wrenched hard downwards, forcing Nelly's spine to buckle and her face to plummet towards the ground.

'LET GO, I SAID!' screamed Nelly, thrashing about with her arms in attempt to gain hold of Asti's wrist. 'LET GO OF MY PONYTAIL NOW!'

Asti's eyes glowered. With the aggression of a hammer thrower she spun Nelly full circle by her ponytail, and then ejected her full tilt and headlong into the sports hall wall.

Nelly crunched into the wall and then crumpled three ways at once. Her knees buckled, her neck jolted and her brain rattled.

Before she knew it, Asti was upon her again.

'TELL EVERYONE I HAD THE SQUITS, DID YOU?' screeched Asti, jumping on to Nelly's shoulders and toppling her to the ground.

'MADE ME A LAUGHING STOCK IN FRONT OF THE WHOLE SCHOOL, HAVE YOU?' screamed Asti, pushing Nelly's face into the grass in an attempt to make her eat dirt.

Nelly's mind reeled. One minute she had been

peeling a banana, the next she was being taken apart herself.

'I DIDN'T TELL ANYONE!' she squawked, her cheek pressed flat to the ground. 'I ONLY TOLD CRAIG!'

'OH, GREAT!' spat Asti, thumping her sister between the shoulder blades, and then bombing low and hard into the small of Nelly's back with her knees. 'YOU ONLY TOLD ONE OF DARREN LEADBETTER'S BEST FRIENDS!'

Nelly winced. That hurt.

'HOW DID I KNOW CRAIG WAS GOING TO SAY SOMETHING!' she protested, flattening her palms to the turf and then jacking Asti's body upwards in an attempt to throw her off.

Asti toppled from Nelly's back and fell to the ground herself. Before she could relaunch her attack, Nelly had set upon her.

'SEE HOW YOU LIKE IT!' screamed Nelly, lunging for the back of Asti's hair but finding no ponytail to grab.

Asti's face pinched painfully as a fistful of bob was wrenched from its roots.

'SEE HOW YOU LIKE THIS!' she screamed, twisting her shoulders sharply and launching her nail extensions in the direction of Nelly's face.

'FIGHT! FIGHT! FIGHT! FIGHT! FIGHT! FIGHT! FIGHT! FIGHT!' exploded a gladiatorial chorus from the playground.

Word of the warring sisters had spread to the dinner queue and the entire population of the assembly hall seemed to have dropped what they were doing to witness the spectacle.

'FIGHT FIGHT FIGHT FIGHT!' clapped the spectators.

Nelly ran her hand down her cheek and checked her fingertips, oblivious to the baying crowds of pupils that had circled around her and her sister.

Asti had drawn blood. Asti was dead meat.

With a banshee scream, Nelly swung her arm like a haymaker and slapped her sister flat across the jaw. Asti's head lurched to one side, and then came back at Nelly, eyes blazing. In a flash, the two sisters' blazers, school trousers and school shoes became locked in a tornado of kicks, bites and scratches.

Craig was the first to intervene, forcing his way through the crowds, and diving into the fray in a valiant but futile attempt to pull the sisters apart.

Mr Sturgiss was the second person to intervene.

'ENOUGH!' he bellowed, his eyes burning and his face purple with rage.

The sea of spectators parted in an instant as the headmaster strode like a one-man riot squad into the circle and lifted both girls from the ground by the collars of their blazers.

'MY OFFICE NOW!' he hollered, fixing Nelly, Asti and Craig in turn with an apocalyptic frown.

'But—' said Craig.

'NOW!' boomed the headmaster.

Nelly and Asti

stared shamefaced at the floor, rubbing dirt, grass and squashed banana from their blazers and trousers.

The baying crowds had evaporated the instant the headmaster had turned up, and the silence that surrounded them now left both girls with a strange feeling of anticlimax.

'I'll finish you off later,' growled Asti out of the corner of her mouth.

'NOW!' boomed Mr Sturgiss.

Nelly abandoned her banana, returned her crumpled Tupperware to her school bag and joined the single-file funeral march across the playground in the direction of the headmaster's office. Apart from a surprise entry in her monster sitting diary, the day had been an unmitigated disaster.

She had squashed banana all over her blazer.

Thanks to Asti.

She still hadn't asked Craig if he wanted to come to the Wattwatts on Saturday.

Thanks to Asti.

Now Craig was in trouble too.

Thanks to Asti.

Who knows, maybe Craig would finish with her after all this?

All thanks to Asti.

'I hate her,' thought Nelly, running her fingertip gingerly across the scratch that Asti's nail extensions had added to her face.

'If Craig finishes with me, I will totally totally finish her.'

6

'FIGHTING?!

'FIGHTING EACH OTHER? IN THE SCHOOL PLAYGROUND!'

Nelly's mum lowered the letter from Mr Sturgiss, reread it, lowered it again and then slammed it furiously down on to the kitchen table.

Nelly and Asti stood forlornly in the kitchen and waited for worse to come.

They had returned from school that evening in stone-faced silence. Having been executed by their headmaster at lunchtime, the time had come for them to be guillotined by their mum.

'THREE HOURS' DETENTION! THREE DETENTIONS AFTER SCHOOL! FOR FIGHTING? EACH OTHER! IN THE PLAYGROUND!' growled their mum, repeating each crime with the solemnity of a news reporter.

'BUT YOU'RE SISTERS!' she gasped. 'TWIN SISTERS!!'

Nelly and Asti stared at the floor tiles. They were a little less intimidating than their mum.

'Twin sisters are supposed to get on, not FIGHT!' glared their mum. 'And especially not fight at school, in the playground. What must everybody think?'

Asti and Nelly decided silence was the best answer.

'Three hours' detention! You're lucky you weren't expelled!' raged their mum.

Nelly tucked her hands behind her back. She had decided to keep schtum about the other detention she had been given that day.

'Nelly got another hour's detention for being late to school this morning,' said Asti, spitefully deflecting her mum's anger towards her sister.

Nelly wilted. Asti must have overheard her talking to Craig outside the headmaster's office.

'WHAT!' fumed their mum. 'Three hours' detention for fighting in the playground isn't enough for you, Petronella?'

Nelly wilted again. She hated being called Petronella.

'How many more hours' detention have you got that you weren't going to tell me about?' glared her mum, placing her hands on her hips and boring into the top of Nelly's bowed head with her eyes.

'I've got one hour on Monday after school for being late,' replied Nelly sheepishly.

'TRUANCY AND FIGHTING WITH YOUR SISTER IN THE PLAYGROUND! HOW PERFECTLY SPLENDID!' snapped her mum. 'WHAT A PERFECTLY SPLENDID APPROACH TO YOUR EDUCATION THAT IS!'

Asti lowered her head and concealed a smirk. Her deflection tactic seemed to be working beautifully.

'AND I DON'T KNOW WHAT YOU'RE SMIRKING AT, ASTILBE!' stomped her mum. 'It's a wonder your sister isn't late for school more than she is, the amount of time you spend in the bathroom!'

Asti swapped her smirk for a frown.

'And what's that on your blazers?' Their mum glared pointing to the mysterious gooey patches that both girls had tried to erase with their sleeves. 'AND YOUR TROUSERS!'

'Squashed banana,' mumbled Nelly.

Nelly's mum's cheeks inflated like a puffa fish and her outstretched arm redirected to the foot of the stairs.

'Go to your rooms, the two of you, and stay there until your father comes home. We'll see what HE has to say about it!'

With their faces still pointing at the floor, the two girls wheeled out of the kitchen and swapped a view of the floor tiles for a view of the hallway carpet.

A view of the stair carpet led them to a view of the landing carpet where the two sisters silently parted.

Nelly closed the door of her bedroom and stared despondently at the view of her bedroom carpet.

She had never physically fought her sister before. Yes, they had exchanged many an insult but never had they actually come to blows.

She raised herself from her bed and ambled over to her dressing table to examine her face in the mirror. The paler half of her face had a scratch running from her cheek to her chin.

The only good news was that she and Craig were still an item. Despite being handed an hour's detention himself for 'getting involved', Craig had told Nelly on the way home from school that things between them were still cool.

Actually, even better, she had finally got round to inviting him to the Wattwatts and, totally fantastically, he had said yes!

All she had to do now was ask the Wattwatts if it would be OK.

She returned to her bed, and stared at her monster sitting phone. She was too miserable to call them now. Her dad would be home from work in the next hour, and until she had come through her third execution of the day Nelly could muster very little enthusiasm to do anything.

With a sigh and a grimace she flopped on to

her bed and stared at the ceiling.

What was her dad going to say?

'I bet he's going to go mental,' she groaned.

7

Mental was one word for it. DOOLALLY-LA-LA was another.

'FIGHTING!' he fumed. 'FIGHTING! LIKE YOBS IN THE STREET!'

'Right, that's it,' he said, wrenching his tie from his collar and hurling it at the settee. 'It's going to stop and it's going to stop right now! You two have been at each other's throats for days now. I don't know what it's all about and I don't care. All I know is it STOPS RIGHT NOW!'

Nelly and Asti withdrew into the cushions of the settee, and stared shamefaced at views of their laps.

Even their mum squirmed a little uncomfortably at the sight of her husband about to explode.

'I AM FED UP COMING HOME EACH

EVENING AND WALKING INTO AN ATMOSPHERE. IF YOU'RE NOT ARGUING ABOUT ONE THING, YOU'RE ARGUING ABOUT ANOTHER!'

Nelly and Asti kept their eyes rooted to their knees.

'What is the matter with the two of you?' Dad shook. 'I'll tell you what the matter with you is. You're spoilt. You've had it too much your own way for too long. AND IT'S GOING TO STOP, RIGHT HERE, RIGHT NOW!'

Nelly raised her eyes just enough to see her dad's suit jacket go flying across the lounge.

'FOR STARTERS YOU ARE BOTH GROUNDED FOR A MONTH!' he roared. 'FOR SECONDERS, THERE WILL BE NO MORE TAXI SERVICE FROM ME OR YOUR MUM.'

Nelly's heart sunk, and she prepared herself for the worst.

'AND THERE WILL BE NO MORE MONSTER SITTING FOR YOU FOR ONE WHOLE MONTH EITHER!'

'Starting from Sunday,' blurted Nelly. 'Please,

Dad, I've already arranged to visit the Wattwatts on Saturday, it's all arranged and everything!'

'STARTING FROM TONIGHT!' bellowed her dad.

Asti's face switched from a frown to a smirk as Nelly's monster sitting appointment went up in smoke.

Nelly leaped from the sofa, dropped to her knees in front of her dad and wrapped her arms imploringly around his suit trousers. There was more at stake than a visit to the Wattwatts. There was a first date with Craig at stake too.

'PLEAAASSEE, Dad,' she begged. 'It's not the Wattwatts' fault that Asti and I had a fight at school today. It's not fair if you punish them too. They've never been out of their house before, and Saturday is their first chance, it's going to be a really special day for them, and they're sooooo looking forward to it. Wak's a dad just like you, with children just like you, it would be sooooo unfair to punish him and his entire family for something I've done! Please, Dad. PLEASE don't ground me till Sunday. I'll do the washing-up and drying up and everything . . . and I'll water the aloe vera, just don't ground me till Sunday, PLEAAAASE.'

Nelly's dad looked down at the top of his daughter's head and crumbled.

'All right,' he sighed. 'You're both grounded from Sunday.'

Asti's smirk switched back to a frown.

'But I want us both to be grounded from tonight!' she complained, desperate to scupper Nelly's visit to some of her beloved ten-headed freaks.

Nelly turned round and glared at her, but she had no need to worry.

'I have said enough on the matter,' said their dad, struggling now to maintain such high levels of anger.

'Let go of my knees, please, Nelly, and go and make up with your sister.'

Nelly's nervous system juddered with the horror of the suggestion.

'Asti, come and make up with Nelly,' said her dad, drawing his other daughter into the middle of the carpet with the hook of his finger.

The two girls rose simultaneously, Asti from the settee, Nelly from the carpet. With the enthusiasm of two prisoners walking to the gallows the warring sisters met in the middle of the lounge.

'Sorry,' murmured Nelly, raising her hand with the limpness of a beached jellyfish.

'Hugs not handshakes!' growled their mum from the armchair.

An uncomfortable pause followed as the two girls contemplated the impossible. A hug?

After all they'd been through.

'Or the grounding starts TONIGHT!' warned their dad.

Nelly sprung her arm around Asti's back before she could escape, and then trapped her with her other arm.

'That's better!' smiled their mum. 'Isn't that better than fighting each other?'

Nelly and Asti stiffened.

'Now, let's treat this hug as the start of a new dawn,' said her dad, walking to the other side of the lounge to retrieve his suit jacket from the magazine rack. 'Let this hug be the start of a new relationship between the two of you. A relationship that is full of love, trust and understanding. Your mum and I have a special relationship like that, and we're not even twins! For you two it should be easy.'

Nelly counted to twenty to make the hug look convincing, and then unsprang her arms.

Asti stood rigid in the middle of the lounge for a moment and then feigned to kiss Nelly on her scratched cheek.

'War is over!' smiled her dad.

'It's only just begun,' whispered Asti.

8

Nelly had an important phone call to make. She returned to her bedroom, still bristling from the hug that she had been forced to give Asti, changed out of her school uniform and parked herself at her homework desk.

The ticking-off from her dad had been her worst ever, but at least she had managed to salvage her next monster sitting adventure, not to mention her first date with Craig.

'I do hope they say yes,' she thought, picking up the phone and dialling the Wattwatts number.

After two rings and a crackle, Wak answered the phone.

'Wak Wattwatt, what what?' he crackled.

'Nelly Morton,' said Nelly, resisting the urge to add a 'what what'.

'Hello, Nelly!' Wak hummed. 'All set for Saturday, what what?'

Nelly twiddled the phone cord around her finger and then went for it.

'Yes, I am thank you, Wak. I'm really looking forward to meeting you and your family. It's always a delight to meet monsters, in fact it's such a delight I was wondering if you would possibly mind if I brought a friend with me to meet you too?'

There was a pause, followed by some muffled crackles and a low hum.

'I don't see why not,' returned the voice. 'Any friend of Nelly the Monster Sitter is a friend of ours, what what!'

Nelly's heart bounced.

'He's ever such a nice friend!' she beamed. 'His name's Craig and he goes to the same school as me. I think he's the nicest boy in my year, and I just know you're going to like him too!'

'Can't wait to meet him, Nelly,' crackled Wak. 'Make sure he brings some rubber gloves.'

Nelly shifted in her seat. She had completely

forgotten about the rubber gloves.

'I . . . will,' she faltered.

'How many fingers do you have, by the way?' crackled Wak.

Nelly looked down at her free hand. She had been so thrown by the rubber gloves, she needed to remind herself. 'Five on each hand, including my thumbs,' she answered.

'How interesting!' crackled Wak. 'The children will be surprised!'

Nelly stared at both of her hands for a moment and then shook her head. Her hands didn't look very surprising to her.

'Please feel free to bring your special friend on Saturday, Nelly, but please make sure you both wear rubber gloves!'

'We will,' murmured Nelly, more than a little intrigued. 'See you Saturday, Wak.'

'Will do, what what!' crackled Wak. 'Rubber gloves and all!'

Nelly replaced the receiver and sat in silence for a moment. Craig *was* allowed to accompany her to the Wattwatts. That was good news. But he'd have to wear rubber gloves. How would he feel about that? In all the teen mags Nelly had read, she'd never seen a first date that included rubber gloves.

'Wattwatts must be really slimy, not spiky,' she thought. 'Maybe they're extra slimy slimy.'

She pulled her monster sitting diary towards her, and blinked at the entry she had scribbled down that morning.

'Maybe they're not slimy at all,' she smiled. 'Maybe they just want us to do the washing-up!'

Slimy or not? Washing-up or not? Rubber gloves would be compulsory.

'I'd better ring Craig to tell him,' she thought, jumping on to her bed and pulling her mobile phone from her jeans. 'What a first date this is going to be!'

Craig was cool as ever about everything. His mum kept spare packets of rubber gloves under the sink, and he was sure he could relieve her of a pair without her knowing or him explaining.

'Mine are yellow!' laughed Nelly.

'Mmm,' smiled Craig. 'Mine will be purple, I think. We don't want to clash, do we!'

'Are you sure you want to come?' said Nelly, crossing her fingers. 'We could just walk into town instead maybe. Dad says the ambulance drivers are going to do a march down the high street. We could go and watch them, if you like,' she said, praying that he wouldn't like at all.

'What, and miss out on my first monsters!'

exclaimed Craig. 'I can see ambulance drivers any time!' he laughed.

'Except when they're on strike!' giggled Nelly.

'You know what I mean!' laughed Craig.

'How are you with slime?' asked Nelly, smiling up at her bedroom ceiling.

'Well, I don't like school dinners,' chuckled Craig.

'Not that sort of slime,' laughed Nelly. 'I mean slug sort of slime. I think the Wattwatts might be a bit like giant slugs. That's why they've asked us to take rubber gloves.'

'I used to race snails once,' said Craig. 'Trod on my fastest one by mistake. That was pretty slimy. And bubbly. I was OK though. I gave it a proper burial and everything . . . without gloves.'

'Mmm,' frowned Nelly. Craig's experience of slime was a bit low volume, but he seemed keen enough.

'I could take some antiseptic wipes as well, if you like,' said Craig. 'My mum keeps loads of those under the sink too.'

'I'm not sure that's a good idea,' said Nelly. 'It

might look a bit rude.'

'We could tell them they're hankies!' chuckled Craig.

'Errr, I think not,' smiled Nelly. 'Let's just stick with the rubber gloves.'

Over the next two hours, the topic of their phone conversation meandered from monsters, to Asti, to parents, to being grounded, to headmasters, to school friends, to Saturday, to teacakes and back to monsters again.

'It's Friday tomorrow!' said Nelly. 'Only one day to go!'

'See you tomorrow, what what!' laughed Craig.

'No more detentions, what what!' laughed Nelly.

9

Friday passed by both slowly and strangely for Nelly. No words were exchanged between her and Asti at breakfast, although both girls were quick to appear sugar sweet each time their parents glanced their way.

Asti vacated the bathroom in alarmingly good time and, even more strangely, left for school a good half an hour earlier than was necessary.

Although her motives were unclear, it was obvious to Nelly that Asti was planning something.

Whatever Asti was up to, it didn't materialize at school. There were no more fights in the playground, there were plenty of scowls in the corridor, but there was nothing of any real substance to furnish Nelly with a clue.

Apart from huddles.

On three occasions at least, when Nelly spotted

Asti in school she appeared at the centre of a huddle. The huddles varied in size, from three to five girls, but other than that there was little or nothing to be gleaned.

'She's up to something,' said Nelly, passing Craig half a banana at lunchtime.

'She's definitely up to something,' she murmured to herself as she trudged into the assembly hall at the end of the day to serve her first detention.

'Whatever it is, it's costing her,' said Craig, meeting her outside the school gates one hour later. 'That's the third girl I've seen her handing money to.'

Nelly peered back along the line of the school fence. Asti was huddling yet again.

'Money?' frowned Nelly. 'How much money?'

'I don't know,' said Craig. 'We're too far away to see, but she definitely took something out of her purse.'

'Perhaps she's buying some new friends!' laughed Nelly. 'It's the only way she's ever going to get some!'

'Don't be horrible,' said Craig. 'Remember what you said. She's your sister, don't forget.'

Nelly stood, or rather ambled, corrected.

'Did you tell her that Darren fancies her?' asked Craig.

'NO, I DID NOT!' replied Nelly.

'Why not?' asked Craig.

'WHY DO YOU THINK!' exclaimed Nelly.

'Point taken,' smiled Craig. 'I've got my rubber gloves ready,' he said, changing the subject. 'I've hidden them under my mattress.'

'Mine are still in the kitchen drawer,' said Nelly. 'We've only got one pair, so I can't swipe them till the last minute.'

'How are we going to get to Jamboree Grove?' asked Craig, turning into Brittle Street.

'Argh,' frowned Nelly, releasing Craig's hand and turning to face him. 'I forgot to tell you. We're going to have to walk, I'm afraid. My mum and dad have stopped my lifts for a month, starting yesterday. My dad normally taxis me to my monsters' houses, but I don't think he will tomorrow. I'll try and persuade him, but I'm pretty sure he won't.'

'Walking to Jamboree Grove is cool,' he said with a smile.

'Cool,' said Nelly, slipping her hand into his again. 'Why don't we meet at the top of Candy Close at one o'clock? That should give us plenty of time to get there.'

'Sounds cool to me,' said Craig. 'Do you want me to be wearing my rubber gloves when I meet you?' He chuckled.

'Errr, NO!' laughed Nelly. 'Let's save those for the Wattwatts!'

The two friends parted at the bottom of Fountain Street, with a firm date and arrangements in place.

'YOU'RE SURE I WON'T HAVE TO RHYME ANYTHING?' Craig shouted with a parting wave.

'I'M SURE!' Nelly waved back. 'JUST DON'T FORGET YOUR GLOVES!'

As the back of Craig's blazer disappeared from view, Nelly's thoughts returned to Asti. More specifically to the huddles.

'She's definitely definitely definitely up to

something,' she murmured. 'And if it's costing her money, it's something major.'

Instead of going up to her bedroom to change when she got home, Nelly hovered by the window of the lounge. Not only had Asti left for school half an hour early that morning, she was two hours late returning home.

'What are you up to?' asked Nelly with a suspicious frown, as Asti finally stepped through the front door.

Asti dumped her school bag at the foot of the stairs, and slipped her blazer coolly from her shoulders.

'That's for me to know, and you to find out,' she sneered.

10

Nelly kept her distance until the following morning, when the weekend frying pan and a carton of fresh orange juice brought both sisters to the kitchen table for brunch.

Nelly's efforts to persuade her dad to taxi her and Craig to Jamboree Grove had fallen on deaf ears, and now an attempt to persuade her mum was about to fail miserably too.

'No more lifts for a month, Nelly. That's what your father and I have decided upon, and that is precisely what we are going to stick to,' said her mum, wafting a forkful of fried tomato in front of Nelly's face as she spoke.

'And anyway, I'm not going anywhere near the high street today. Those wretched ambulance men will jam the road up with their march.'

Nelly stabbed a piece of bacon with her fork

and finally gave up the cause. A walk to Jamboree Grove it would be.

She chewed and slurped and munched and crunched through brunch, casting covert glances at Asti whenever opportunities came her way.

Even in the absence of a huddle, Asti looked suspicious.

'Make sure you leave the Wattwatts' address and telephone number on the mirror,' said her dad, reaching across the table with his fork to snaffle the bacon bones both daughters had pushed to one side of their plates.

'I will,' said Nelly.

'And make sure you're back by six,' said her mum, flattening another steaming tinned tomato on to her toast with the back of her fork.

'I will,' said Nelly.

Nelly, Asti and their mum listened in silence as Dad satisfied his carnivorous tendencies with a crunching demolition of the bacon bones.

'And what have you got planned for yourself today, Asti?' Dad asked, prising a tiny white bone fragment from his back teeth.

Asti looked up from her plate and reached casually for the orange juice carton.

'This and that,' she said, keeping her cards up her sleeve.

Nelly frowned inwardly. She didn't like the sound of 'this' and she didn't like the sound of 'that'.

'Well, make the most of the day,' said her mum, 'because your grounding starts tomorrow.'

'Oh, I will,' smirked Asti, pouring and downing a glass of orange juice in one action and then sliding from the kitchen stool.

'I'll wash up!' said Nelly, anxious to lay claim to the rubber gloves early. 'And I'll dry,' she said, in the half hope that her dad would see her for the truly dutiful daughter she was, and change his mind about the taxi offer.

No such luck.

'Asti can dry,' said her mum. 'Asti, give Nelly a hand clearing up.'

Asti and Nelly swapped poisonous glances, and then formed an unholy alliance at the sink.

Two taps, one bottle of washing-up liquid, four

plates, four knives, four forks, one Pyrex bowl, one frying pan and absolutely zero words later, they parted at the kitchen door and went their increasingly separate ways.

Nelly's separate way took her into the lounge. Asti's upstairs to her room.

'What's she up to?' thought Nelly. 'What IS she up to?'

She dumped herself in an armchair and looked at her watch. It was quarter past twelve. She was dressed and ready for her visit and had little else to do but wait. With an impatient fidget she shifted over on to one buttock, and patted the back pocket of her green jeans. The rubber gloves were tucked inside, both rolled up and folded, like a cross between a cigar and a pastry.

Nelly ran her fingertips across them and then pulled them out of her pocket.

'I'll put them in my front pockets,' she thought, glancing at the door to check that no one was coming, and then unfurling and separating them in turn.

'They'll be less noticeable if I separate them,' she murmured to herself. 'Less of a bulge.'

With the one bigger bulge divided into two, Nelly switched her attentions to the lounge window. At least it was a beautiful day. The sun was shining, the skies looked clear, it would be the perfect afternoon for a walk. Even a long walk.

Judging from the sounds coming from the back garden, her dad had decided it was the perfect day to cut the grass. Or rather her mum had decided it was the perfect day to tell her husband it was the perfect day to cut the grass.

Nelly toyed with the TV remote control but then dropped it on to the lounge carpet. She was too excited to watch telly.

She craned her head in the direction of the hallway mirror.

'I know what I'll do,' she smiled. 'I'll write the Wattwatts' details on a Post-it, stick the Post-it on the hall mirror, and leave early! After all, it's far too nice a day to be stuck in here!'

And with that she rose from the armchair,

pulled a felt tip from the sideboard, did the necessaries with the Post-it and stepped quickly out of the front door.

'I hope Craig doesn't stand me up,' she thought, stepping into the Saturday afternoon sunshine, and skipping down the path.

She closed the front gate behind her and turned excitedly into Sweet Street. Candy Close was six streets further along.

'He's already there!' she gasped, peering down the road to see a small but familiar figure toe-poking a stone across Sweet Street. She was right. Craig had left his house early too, and had been waiting at the end of Sweet Street for some five minutes or more!

'He must be keen!' thought Nelly. 'OOPS!' she faltered, 'I forgot to tell Mum and Dad I was leaving!'

She glanced back at her house just in time to see the face of her sister disappear behind the curtains of her mum and dad's bedroom.

'They'll work out where I've gone,' she thought, sticking her tongue out at the curtains and then turning back in Craig's direction.

'Really keen!' she thought, skipping down the street with a wave of her hand.

11

As long walks went, this one went particularly well. In fact it trounced any long walk Nelly had ever taken before by a mile. She and Craig were a good match, sharing similar senses of humour and an interest in monsters, not to mention pairs of rubber gloves.

In reality it was a long deliberate dawdle rather than a walk.

An hour and a half was more than enough time to get to the Wattwatts' house, and by the time Nelly and Craig turned into Jamboree Grove, their first date had taken them the length and breadth of the high street, and halfway round the precinct too.

They had bumped into Josh Waites and Colin Lampton outside the kebab house. This according to Craig was 'cool' for two reasons.

One because Josh and Col were cool, and two because being seen together in the high street at the weekend officially made Nelly and Craig an item.

After the week she'd had and the day she was having, Nelly could conservatively have awarded her life a cool score of about ten zillion.

'Here we are are!' she smiled, releasing Craig's hand to check her watch.

It was five to two.

'Should we put our rubber gloves on now?' asked Craig, scanning the crescent-like curve of Jamboree Grove.

'I think we'll look a bit silly if we do,' said Nelly, 'especially on a summery day like today!'

'You're the expert,' laughed Craig, tucking his purple gloves back into his pocket.

'Let's knock on the door first, and see what they say,' said Nelly, stepping up the pace a little in case the Wattwatts' house was at the end of the curved road.

'Are you nervous?' asked Craig, increasing his speed to keep up. 'I am a bit.'

'Noooooooooo,' laughed Nelly, 'there's nothing to be nervous about! All the monsters I have met have been lovely! Apart from the Tooth Furry. I'll tell you about him another day. Remember, if it's a purple door, it means they've got four heads!'

Craig looked at the plain white door of number 24 and kept walking.

There were lots of cars parked along the kerbside of the Grove, each allocated a private parking space of its own. Presumably all the car owners were in their back gardens, driving lawnmowers to and fro instead.

The front gardens of the Jamboree Grove houses were small but neatly kept. The houses themselves were new builds, with matching windows and doors that their owners had had little time to alter.

Nelly liked the look of new houses. The clean yellow bricks gave them a fresh and inviting appearance, and the iron railings that fronted each garden were gold-tipped and rust-free.

'Forty-four,' counted Craig as they approached

the middle of the Grove. 'They must live further along.'

'That'll be them,' said Nelly, pointing further round the bend to the only kerb space missing a parked car. 'The Wattwatts won't have a car. That'll be their house over there.'

There were six more houses to go. 'Shall we put our rubber gloves on yet?' said Craig, slipping his fingertips into his pockets.

'Not yet!' laughed Nelly. 'Let's say hello to them first!'

Craig nodded and slipped just one of his hands into his pocket.

'Fifty-six,' said Nelly, with a glance at her watch. 'I told you this one would be fifty-six.' She pointed to the gap between the parked cars. 'Come on,' she said, unlatching the small wrought-iron gate. 'It's seventeen seconds to two o'clock!'

Craig dropped into Nelly's slipstream. He didn't know what to expect, he didn't know how to behave. The safest thing, he had decided, was to just follow Nelly.

Nelly's eager footsteps led them to the

Wattwatts' front door. To Craig's secret relief, its panels were glossed red and not purple.

'I'd rather build up to four heads,' he thought to himself. 'Hopefully it'll be one head, or maybe two.'

Nelly lifted the zigzagged door knocker of number 56 and rapped hard.

'Just do what I do,' she whispered as the door opened wide.

Craig nodded, and then gulped.

For there, standing on the doormat of a house in the middle of an estate in which he himself lived . . . was a monster! The first monster he had ever seen in his life.

It wasn't slimy, it wasn't spiky, it wasn't scaly.

It was shiny.

As shiny as a beetle shell. But it didn't look like an insect.

It was as yellow as a canary but it didn't look like a bird.

Its arms and legs were impossibly angular, with elbows and knees that protruded like rose thorns, or maybe sharks' fins.

But it didn't look like a flower or a fish.

It looked like . . .

. . . a lightning strike.

Its body was zigzagged just like a lightning strike!

And its eyes were fluorescent green.

Nelly beamed excitedly across the front step and extended her arm for a handshake.

'Nelly, Craig,' crackled the monster, extending one of its thin angular arms, but then withdrawing its spiked fingers sharply.

'Rubber gloves! Rubber gloves! You didn't forget your rubber gloves, did you, what what!'

Nelly glanced round at Craig and smiled.

'You were right!' she said, plunging her hands into her pockets and producing a pair of her mum's yellowest and finest. 'We should have put them on before we knocked!'

Craig slipped his hands into his pockets and plucked out his own.

'Excellent!' smiled Wak. 'You wouldn't thank me for whacking you with a thousand volts, what what!'

Nelly manoeuvred her fingers into the fingerholes of her mum's washing-up gloves and then turned wide-eyed to Craig.

'We're electrically charged, Nelly,' grinned the monster. 'All Wattwatts are electrically charged, didn't you know that, what what?!'

Craig stared back at Nelly, and then divebombed his fingers into the purple gloves.

'No need to worry if you're wearing rubber gloves, what what!' smiled Wak, 'Electricity won't pass through rubber gloves! Now then, which one's Nelly and which one's Craig?'

'I'm Nelly,' said Nelly, offering up a yellow rubber glove for a handshake.

'Hello, Nelly, I'm Wak,' said Wak, closing his fingers firmly around Nelly's knuckles.

Nelly tensed slightly, but felt little more than a light pulse of energy passing through her hand.

'And I'm Craig,' said Craig, stepping forward gamely and holding out five purple fingers.

'Nice to meet you, Nelly. Nice to meet you, Craig, what what!' replied Wak, retreating inside the house with a crackle. 'Please do come inside.'

Craig glanced at Nelly. Nelly smiled at Craig.

'It's gonna be fun!' she whispered. 'I promise!'

12

If Nelly and Craig were up for some fun, so were the Wattwatts' children.

There was no hallway to file through, which meant Craig and Nelly had stepped directly into a small open-plan lounge.

Zap, Fusea, Urth and Volta were standing by the chimney breast waiting to greet them.

'Hello, Nelly, hello, Craig, what what!' chorused the children, a pulse of electricity zigzagging upwards through their bodies as they spoke.

'Hello,' dueted Craig and Nelly with simultaneous waves of their rubber gloves.

'Now then, children,' clapped their mother, 'no jumping or climbing on Nelly and Craig: you must only touch them on their gloves. We don't want any more nasty shocks, do we, what what?'

The children took two steps excitedly forward, and then one step obediently back.

'I'm Zap,' smiled the children's mother, curtseying politely on yellow thorn-shaped knees.

'I'm Nelly,' curtseyed Nelly.

'And I'm Craig.' Craig smiled, resisting a curtsey and opting for a much cooler nod.

'Please do make yourselves comfortable,' crackled Zap. 'Please treat our home as your own.'

Nelly and Craig scanned the sleek red furniture of the Wattwatts' living room. It was as shiny as their front door and as contoured as a Ferrari bonnet.

'We'll sit here,' said Nelly, nodding Craig in the direction of a two-seater settee moulded from poly carbon.

'And we'll sit here, what what!' crackled Wak, settling next his wife on the three-seater sofa opposite, and then drawing all three children on to both laps for a group hug. 'I must say, Nelly and Craig, it's very kind of you to come.'

'No problem,' coughed Craig, trying to pretend that monsters were pretty much a daily occurrence in his life.

'It's our pleasure!' said Nelly with a smile, glancing covertly at the ceilings floors and walls.

At first covert glance, second covert glance, third covert glance and fourth covert glance, there were no electrical sockets or fittings to be seen.

'Zap and I are so much looking forward to going out for a few hours,' crackled Wak.

Nelly put her rubber glove on Craig's knee, and frowned.

There were no electrical leads on the TV either.

'We thought we'd go pylon-hugging!' crackled Zap. 'When we were moving to the Grove from our last address, we passed some tremendously impressive electricity pylons on the outskirts of town. Stretched right across the fields they did!'

'Over by the golf course, you mean,' said Craig, crossing his legs and starting to feel remarkably at home.

'That's right,' crackled Wak. 'One could

almost feel the life force in them as we drove past.'

'We're terribly fond of nature,' crackled Zap.

Nelly looked at Craig and smiled broadly. She'd heard of hippies tree-hugging, but Zappies pylon-hugging was a new one on both of them.

'Where did you live before?' Craig asked boldly.

'Symchester,' replied Wak. 'We were very happy there, but we were forced to move in the end, after a bit of an unfortunate accident.'

Too polite to ask the obvious, Nelly and Craig looked enquiringly into each of the family members' green fluorescent eyes and waited to be illuminated.

'We took the children swimming,' crackled Wak, 'to the public baths.'

'All they did was jump in . . .' sighed Zap

'And bang!' crackled Wak, throwing his arms up into the air. 'Thirty-six swimmers floating unconscious on the surface!'

'One woman lost her eyebrows,' sighed Zap.

'We had to move house after that, what what!'

Craig put his rubber glove on top of Nelly's rubber glove and looked quizzically at the Wattwatts' three children.

'How many volts do you carry?' he asked. 'If you don't mind me asking,' he added.

'Up to ten thousand,' crackled Wak. 'We can turn our voltage up and down by twisting our ears.'

Nelly and Craig watched as the Wattwatts' children charmingly obliged with an ear-twisting demonstration of their own.

'Twenty volts,' crackled Urth.

'Forty volts,' crackled Fusea.

'Sixty volts,' hummed Volta.

'The children have a much lower voltage than we parents,' crackled Wak. 'It will increase as they get older.'

'Still, better to play safe with the gloves!' smiled Zap.

Nelly and Craig sat transfixed on the two-seater sofa. Before them sat a family of monsters with bright-yellow bodies shaped like lightning bolts, ears that twisted like radio dials, and enough voltage between them to power the national grid.

'I said it would be fun!' whispered Nelly.

'This isn't fun,' whispered Craig, 'it's wild!'

13

'The minibus is here!' shouted Asti, glaring at her watch face and then barging through a huddle of school friends that had gathered on the driveway outside her home.

'About time too!' she fumed, picking a megaphone up from the driveway and stomping out on to the pavement to confront the taxi driver.

'You're late!' she fumed, boring her eyes through the open driver window.

'Sorry, luv,' said the minibus driver, 'the ambulance drivers are marching through town, the high street is shut off and the roads around it are totally gridlocked.'

Asti's knuckles tightened around the handle of her megaphone.

'Where is it you want to go?' asked the minibus driver.

'Fifty-six Jamboree Grove,' snarled Asti, screwing Nelly's Post-it note into a ball, and hurling it at the pavement.

'It's gonna take a while,' said the driver.

'Cut through Caramel Way,' growled Asti.

'Gridlocked,' said the driver.

'Cut though Sherbert Street and up on to the Canal Road,' retorted Asti.

'Chocka,' said the minibus driver with a rueful shake of his head. 'It's gonna take a while and it's gonna cost a few quid too. Sorry, but a gridlock's a gridlock. There's nothing I can do about it.'

'Just drive, will you!' Asti glared at him, determined her masterplan wouldn't be thwarted at the last moment by a bunch of striking ambulance men. She had enough Christmas money to pay for ten minibuses if she needed.

'Can we put our banners in the back?' she asked, flapping her hands at the other girls to hurry them on to the bus.

The minibus driver leaned out of his window on to the pavement side and then frowned as each girl in turn stooped low to the ground and lifted a protest banner from a pile on the driveway.

'You're not joining the march, are you?' frowned the driver.

'No, we're not,' flounced Asti. 'We're forming a march of our own!'

'In Jamboree Grove?' quizzed the driver.

'YES! In JAMBOREE GROVE!' growled Asti.

The minibus driver closed his jaw, dropped his shoulders and stepped out of the minibus with a sigh.

'How many banners have you got?' he frowned.

'All that we'll need!' cackled Asti.

14

It was time for Wak and Zap to leave their home. Electricity pylons beckoned and it was already half past two.

Nelly and Craig stood on the doorstep of the Wattwatts' home and waved Wak and Zap down the pathway.

'Give our love to the pylons!' shouted Nelly.

'Hug one for me!' laughed Craig.

Wak and Zap waved cheerily back at the doorstep and then strode off in the direction of some serious volts.

Nelly closed the front door behind them and turned back into the Wattwatts' living room. The children were seated expectantly on the edge of the three-seater sofa.

'What do we do now?' asked Craig with a waggle of his purple fingers.

'We play games!' smiled Nelly. 'That's what we do now!'

Urth, Volta and Fusea inched further forward, but resisted the temptation to launch themselves headlong at their guests.

'We play *safe* games,' said Nelly, looking thoughtfully at her rubber fingers. 'Now then, what kind of safe games can we play?'

'We could play pat-a-cake!' suggested Craig, raising his purple gloves before his chest and going through the motions.

'What a good idea!' Nelly smiled. 'You should go monster sitting more!'

Craig smiled. High praise indeed, coming from the only monster sitter in the land!

'Pat-a-cake it is!' said Nelly drawing the children from the sofa and positioning them in a straight line.

'Shall we kneel?' said Craig, keen to impart his next useful monster sitting suggestion.

'I think we should,' said Nelly dropping down to Fusea's eye level.

'Now there's three of you and two of us,' said

Nelly, 'so I need a volunteer to wait their turn.'

Volta raised her hand. 'I'm the oldest, I'll wait my turn,' she crackled.

Nelly and Craig shuffled across the floor on their knees and then prepared to start.

'Have you ever played pat-a-cake before?' asked Nelly, suspecting the answer would be no.

'No,' blinked the children.

'OK then,' she said, shuffling round to face Craig. 'Watch Craig and me and we'll show you how to do it.'

Craig raised the flats of his hand and smiled. The last time he'd played pat-a-cake he must have been about five.

Nelly gave him a wink and patted her palms against his.

'Pat-a-cake pat-a-cake baker's man,' she sang.
'Bake me a cake as fast as you can
Prick it and prod it and mark it with C
And put it in the oven for Craig and me.'

The three children watched in earnest as the

rubber-gloved palms of Nelly and Craig slapped and clapped before them.

'Our turn!' crackled Fusea, jumping to the front of the queue.

Craig and Nelly shuffled round on their knees and divided their attention between Fusea and Urth.

With every pat, slap and clap the smiles on the two children grew wider.

'This is fun!' crackled Urth.

'My turn next,' hummed Volta, jumping in front of Craig the instant Fusea had marked her cake with an F.

'Do you play this a lot, what what?' she asked, slapping her three-fingered palms against the flattened palms of Craig's purple gloves.

'Errr . . . all the time!' fibbed Craig, not wanting to undermine the excitement of the occasion.

Nelly turned to him with a smile. 'All the way home from school!' she laughed.

The pat-a-cake rotation continued between the three children for a further fifteen minutes or more before Nelly drew a halt to the proceedings with a final clap and slap of her gloves.

'Time for another game,' she laughed.

'What's an oven?' asked Volta, perching her zigzagged bottom on the edge of the red moulded sofa. 'We know what cakes are, but what's an oven?'

Craig offered up a simple explanation. 'An oven is something people cook cakes in,' he said.

'It's electric just like you,' added Nelly.

'Or gas,' put in Craig.

'The electricity heats up the cake mixture and browns the cakes off until they are perfectly cooked and ready to eat.'

The three Wattwatt children looked quizzically at each other and then peered at the palms of their hands.

'We don't use ovens,' crackled Volta, raising the flats of her circular palms to Nelly and Craig's noses. 'We use our hands to cook our food.'

'Wattwatts like current buns!' crackled Fusea.

Nelly and Craig peered down their noses at Volta's outstretched hands and then jumped as the inner circles of the Wattwatts' palms began to rotate like microwave plates.

'Can you feel the heat building?' crackled Volta, with a clockwise twist of his left ear.

'Cool!' said Craig as warm air wafted in the direction of his nostrils.

'I can make it hotter if you like,' crackled Volta, with another twist of her ear.

Craig turned to Nelly, his eyebrows steaming.

Electric monsters with ears that turned, plus PALMS that turned and cooked current buns? How exciting was this!

'What else can Wattwatts do?' asked Craig,

returning to the two-seater sofa.

'Yes, tell us!' urged Nelly, rising from her knees and plonking herself down by his side. 'Just how clever are you?'

15

'C'MON C'MON!' growled Asti. 'We're never going to get there at this rate!'

The minibus she was travelling in had barely travelled at all. After making good progress out of Sweet Street, and fair progress into Praline Avenue, it had ground to a complete halt at the top of Rock Street.

'I told you, luv,' sighed the driver. 'It's gonna be gridlock all the way.'

Asti thumped the glass of the passenger window and then turned towards the back of the bus. Ten of her school friends were occupying the other available seats and all of them were beginning to grow a bit restless.

Actually, 'school friends' was a little bit of an exaggeration. With the exception of Natalie Dupré, they were mercenaries. Asti had bribed them all with her Christmas money to come to her house that morning, and she would be paying them hard cash to join the protest march she had planned.

'We're not getting very far, are we?' complained Natalie, leaning forward in her seat and pressing her lips to Asti's ear.

'Tell me something I DON'T KNOW, PLEASE!' snapped Asti, lifting her foot and slamming it against the glove compartment.

'Feet down, please!' growled the minibus driver, who was starting to get a little hot and bothered himself.

Asti lowered her foot with a haughty shrug.

'The girls want to be paid overtime if we're not back in Sweet Street by five o'clock,' whispered Natalie, obliging with something Asti didn't know and didn't particularly want to hear either.

'I'm already paying them ten pounds each!' snapped Asti, glaring at another queue of cars that the minibus driver was doing his best to join.

'You're only paying me a pound!' frowned Natalie.

'That's because you're a friend!' snarled Asti. 'If you'd been a real friend, you wouldn't even have wanted a pound!'

Natalie slumped back in her seat and then leaned forward again to deliver some more bad news.

'They want time and a half too after five o'clock,' she whispered. 'That means you have to pay them half as much again as the normal ra—'

'I know what time and a half means, thank you!' said Asti, slamming her foot against the glove compartment again, but this time refusing to move it.

'Either your foot comes off, or the lot of you get off,' growled the driver, inching forward out of Rock Street, and then blocking the road until another car conceded him the space to swing on to Loveheart Lane.

Asti dropped her foot again, and then turned to the back of the minibus. If she was paying for everyone to be there, she may as well get her money's worth out of them.

'OK, everyone.' She clapped her hands.

'It's rehearsal time. Does everyone remember their chants?'

The minibus erupted with a raucous cheer as the girls prepared to practise their vocals.

'WHAT DO WE WANT?' shouted Asti.

'DEATH TO MONSTERS!' shouted the girls.

'WHEN DO WE WANT IT?' grinned Asti.

'NOOOOOOOWWWWWWWWWWWWW!!!!' whooped the crowd.

Asti smiled at Natalie. It was ten out of ten for the first chant.

'GIVE US SOME GUNS!' shouted Asti.

'GUNNNNNS!!' chorused the girls.

'GIVE US SOME MONSTERS!'

'MONSTERS!'

'PULL THE TRIGGERS!'

'BANGGGG!' shouted the girls.

'WHAT HAVE WE GOT?' yelled Asti, raising her hands above her head.

'DEAD MONSTERS!!!' cheered the girls.

Natalie's dental brace flashed brightly in the sunshine as her lips broke into a wide and devilish smile. With a few more rehearsals it would be ten out of ten for that chant too.

The minibus driver dropped low into his seat. Oh, how he wished he'd stayed at home. As if being gridlocked by an ambulance strike wasn't enough, he now had another mini protest unfolding behind his headrest.

'ONE MORE TIME!' whooped Asti.

'Never again,' sighed the taxi driver, releasing his hand brake and moving the minibus forward another metre.

16

Back at Jamboree Grove, things just couldn't have been going any better. Nelly and Craig had relaxed back on to the two-seater sofa and had been treated to an amazing display of do-it-yourself electrics.

To light a light bulb, the Wattwatts simply closed their fingers around a solitary bulb and *voilà*! The bulb lit up without any need for a socket, a switch or any kind of electrical connection. The palms of the Wattwatts' hands were the electrical connection!

To clean her teeth, Urth simply needed to grip an electric toothbrush firmly and the head of the brush began to whirr.

To make toast, they simply rotated their ears, sandwiched a slice of bread between their palms and waited for their ear lobes to ping.

'I can see why the swimming baths was such a disaster,' said Nelly, smiling. 'Had your mum and dad taken you out of the house before?'

Volta shook her head. 'That was our first time,' she crackled.

'And our last, what what!' hummed Fusea.

'I'm sure they'll take you out again, when they get to know Lowbridge a bit better,' said Nelly.

'You can go pylon-hugging with them!' added Craig.

'We'd like that.' Urth nodded.

Craig nodded back and ran his eyes from top to zigzagged bottom.

'I'd avoid duck ponds if I were you,' he frowned, conjuring with the image of a boating lake smoking with crispy fried ducks.

'And puddles,' frowned Nelly. 'Puddles could be tricky too.'

'Anything with water in basically,' said Craig. 'Water and electricity can be a pretty dangerous combination.'

'It doesn't stop us having baths, what what!' crackled Fusea.

'We have a bath every night,' fizzed Urth.

'Hot or cold?' asked Nelly, raising her eyes to the ceiling.

'It starts off cold, but we heat it up when we get in it,' crackled Volta.

'We don't need a hot tap, only a cold one,' hummed Urth with a playful twist of her ear.

'What happens when you get in?' asked Nelly,

a little scientifically intrigued.

'A loud bang, basically,' crackled Fusea. 'The bath goes bang, the water starts to steam, and all our dirty bits drop off.'

'No need for soap then?' asked Craig.

'What's soap?' asked Urth, her fluorescent-green eyes blinking quizzically.

'A child's worst nightmare,' laughed Craig.

'What's a nightmare?' crackled Volta.

'Getting into a bath with a Wattwatt,' chuckled Nelly.

The three Wattwatt children smiled. The conversation was leaving them behind a little now.

'What game can we play now?' crackled Fusea.

Nelly looked at her watch. It was a quarter to four.

'It's a lovely day outside,' she smiled. 'Shall we go and play in the garden?'

'Yes, please, what what!' chorused the children.

'There aren't any paddling pools or puddles out there, are there?' chuckled Craig, rising from the sofa, and following Nelly and the children through to the kitchen.

'Lots of gadgets though!' laughed Urth.

'We work them with our electricity!' crackled Volta.

'I can believe it,' laughed Nelly.

17

'What will Nelly do when she sees us?' grinned Natalie.

The latest protest-chant rehearsals had ended with a resounding double cheer and the minibus seemed finally to be on its way.

'She'll go ape!' grinned Asti. 'She's going to die of embarrassment!'

'Serves her right,' said Natalie. 'I'd hate to have someone like her for a sister.'

Asti lifted her foot on to the glove compartment, lowered it immediately and then switched her attention to her watch. It was almost four o'clock.

'TWO HOURS!' she groaned. 'It's taken nearly two hours just to get to Fondant Way! We could have *walked* to Jamboree Grove by now.'

'I don't think the girls would have walked,'

whispered Natalie. 'The banners are a bit too heavy to walk with.'

Asti raised her eyebrows contemptuously. 'Yes, Natalie, I'm sure the ambulance drivers are saying precisely the same thing. Let's not march too far down the high street, because the banners will make our arms ache. I'll tell you what, let's just walk from the chemist's to the butcher's!'

'That's only two shops?' frowned Natalie.

'I KNOW IT'S ONLY TWO SHOPS!' snapped Asti. 'I'M BEING SARCASTIC!'

'I'm only saying,' said Natalie, slumping back into her seat. 'Maybe if you paid them double time, they'd walk.'

'I AM NOT PAYING ANYONE MORE THAN TEN POUNDS!' growled Asti. 'At the rate we're travelling, there will only be time for *one* protest song!'

'We seem to be moving now,' said Natalie, peering out of her window as the minibus drove over crossroads into Sherbert Street.

'I think the high street must be clearing,' said the driver, puffing out his cheeks and moving up to third gear for the first time in over an hour.

'WHAT DO WE WANT?' whooped Asti.

'DEATH TO MONSTERS!' chorused the girls.

'WHEN DO WE WANT IT?!'

'NOOOOOOOOWWWWWWW!!!!!!!!!!!!'

18

The gadgets in the Wattwatts' back garden weren't gadgets in an obvious sense at all.

Both Nelly and Craig had stepped out through the back door expecting to find a garden crossed with a science museum. However it was a swing, slide and roundabout that dominated the neatly mowed lawn.

The swing however was a swing with a difference.

Instead of building momentum with a steady build-up of leg thrusts, the swing in effect swung itself. The Wattwatt children merely had to adjust their ears to the required speed, place their bottoms on the seat and away it went. 'It's easy, what what!' grinned Volta, a pulse of electricity throbbing up the rigid copper cords that suspended the seat from the frame.

'Now watch this!' she crackled, taking one hand off of a cord to twist her ear full circle.

Craig and Nelly stepped back towards the house and stared wide-eyed as the soles of the grinning Wattwatt flew up and over the swing frame in a full 360-degree loop.

'And this!' Volta shouted, adjusting her ear again and then fizzing like a Catherine wheel through the sunshine.

'I hope she's not sick,' said Nelly, slipping her hand into Craig's.

'I hope she can stop it!' gasped Craig, 'If she spins much faster, the swing'll take off.'

'I can spin too!' crackled Urth, racing over to the roundabout and jumping aboard. 'Watch me!' she crackled.

Nelly and Craig switched their attention from the high-speed vertical rotation of the swing to the tornado-like spin of the Wattwatts' miniature roundabout.

'My electricity makes it go round!' crackled Urth, her face a blur of yellow. 'Do you want me to go faster?' she hummed.

'No, that's fast enough!' laughed Nelly, raising her rubber glove and then squeezing Craig's hand anxiously with the other.

'If she lets go she's going to crash straight through the fence!' gasped Craig. 'Look, her eyes have turned into a green line!'

'She won't let go,' reassured Nelly. 'This is normal playtime for a Wattwatt!'

'I'm going on the edils!' crackled Fusea, running across the lawn and placing her bottom at the foot of the slide.

Nelly and Craig looked at each other in puzzlement.

'Here I go!' she crackled, twisting each of her ears in turn and then whizzing upwards from the foot of the slide to top.

'It's a slide backwards!' said Craig with a clap of his rubber gloves. 'An edils is a slide backwards!'

Up and down round and round, over and over the three children flew.

'Where do they get their energy from?' gasped Craig, after twenty minutes of non-stop fairground supersonics.

'I think we know the answer to that question!' laughed Nelly, releasing Craig's hand for a double wave of her gloves.

'ENOUGH, ENOUGH!' she shouted, grabbing both of her ears and motioning the children to slow down.

In the blink of an eye, the play equipment stopped and the children tumbled playfully on to the grass.

'That was fun!' crackled Urth. 'Would you like to have a go!'

Nelly and Craig looked at each other and then raised their gloves simultaneously.

'We'll have to pass, I'm afraid,' said Craig.

The three Wattwatt children settled on the grass within safe distance of their monster sitters' feet, and stretched their zigzagged bodies out into the sunshine.

'It's hot, isn't it!' smiled Nelly, peering up at the sun, and then dropping to crouch on the lawn.

'Not if you turn your temperature down, it isn't!' crackled Fusea with a twist of her ear and a press of her nose.

Nelly chuckled. 'Thermostatic controls too, eh! Tell us what else you can do!'

'Who cuts the grass?' asked Craig, dropping to his knees and running his purple palms over the neatly clipped surface of the lawn.

'Mum does it with the electric scissors,' crackled Volta, leaping to her feet and returning from a small aluminium shed with a pair of garden shears that had the snap of psychotic alligator.

'Put them back!' shouted Nelly, pointing to the shed. 'You'll have someone's head off!'

'I won't!' crackled Volta, a pulse of electricity fizzing from both wrists, right up to the snapping tips of both blades. 'It's only on half speed!'

'We had lots of trees in the garden of our last house,' crackled Urth. 'Would you like to see Dad's chainsaw?'

'NO, WE WOULDN'T!' said Craig, jumping to his feet in alarm. 'I think we should go back into the lounge,' he whispered to Nelly. 'It's a bit high voltage out here!'

'I think you're right,' Nelly whispered back.

'Come on, you three!' she smiled, climbing to her feet. 'You might not be hot, but Craig and I are. Can we go back indoors and get a drink, please!'

'Leru milk!' crackled Fusea, sprinting to the back door. 'Do you like Leru milk?'

Craig gulped without even lifting a glass. 'I guess I'm about to find out,' he wavered.

In the time it took Nelly and Craig to shepherd Fusea and Urth from the garden back into the kitchen, Volta had two long test tubes of Leru milk ready; both exercise-book blue in colour, one exercise-book blue and frothy.

'I fizzed one up, to see if you like it, what what!' grinned Volta holding both test tubes out before her.

Nelly smiled sweetly, took both of the drinks and handed the frothy one to Craig.

'Cheers,' she said, pursing her lips and then raising her test tube to her mouth.

'Cheers,' grimaced Craig, peering into the bubbly blue liquid and then woofing it back down in one.

The three Wattwatt children grinned excitedly, and then frowned at the absence of a bang.

'That was really NICE!' said Craig with a smack of his lips. 'Honestly, that was really really nice!'

He turned to Nelly for confirmation, but found a face frozen with anxiety.

'Excuse me,' frowned Nelly, passing her empty test tube to Urth. 'I need to go somewhere.'

20

Nelly drew back the curtains of the Wattwatts' living room, looked, looked again, and then rocked in her socks with the force of a silent scream.

To her gut-wrenching horror, Asti was standing outside the Wattwatts' front gate, hurling obscenities at the front door through a megaphone. Behind her in the empty car parking space, parading banners backwards and forwards, Natalie Dupré and a huddle of other girls were chanting:

'WHO ATE ALL THE PEOPLE?
WHO ATE ALL THE PEOPLE?
YOU FAT MONSTERS
YOU FAT MONSTERS
YOU ATE ALL THE PEOPLE!'

Nelly's heart dropped into the pit of her stomach, and then the pit of her stomach slid into the toes of her shoes.

'HOW COULD SHE!' she fumed. 'MY OWN SISTER!'

'What is it?' said Craig, entering the lounge with the children.

Nelly's arm sprung up behind her, but it was too late. Before she could stop them from approaching, Craig, Urth, Fusea and Volta had joined her at the window.

The instant the Wattwatt children's faces appeared at the window Asti's hackles rose demonically, and her banner soared into the air.

'MONSTERS OUT!' it read.

On one side.

'MONSTERS DIE!' it screeched from the other.

'What a cow!' said Craig under his breath. 'What an absolute—'

'Language,' ssshed Nelly, slapping a rubber glove to his lips. 'Not in front of the children, please.'

'What are those people saying, Nelly?' said Urth, beginning to feel a little uneasy.

'Never mind what they're saying,' fumed Nelly, wrenching the rubber gloves from her hands.

'Go and sit on the sofa with Craig, while Nelly makes them go away.'

Craig took the signal from Nelly, and coaxed each of the Wattwatt children away from the window.

'You sit on that sofa and I'll sit on this one,' he cautioned, still mindful that even the smallest Wattwatt could give him a lapful of dangerous volts.

Nelly steamed the window with hot breath and pink mist.

'WHAT DO WE WANT?' screamed Asti, dispensing with the megaphone and thrusting her banner high into the afternoon sunshine with both hands.

'DEATH TO MONSTERS!' bayed her mercenaries.

'WHEN DO WE WANT IT!'

'NOWWWWWW!!!!'

Nelly's toes curled and her fists tightened into embittered knots of rage. Here she was, on her first ever date with Craig, monster sitting some of the nicest monster children she'd ever had the pleasure to meet, monster children who had already been forced out of one home . . . and there was Asti, hateful, spiteful, vengeful Asti, screeching and pointing at the house like a witch-finder. Asti, her own sister, her own twin sister, her own flesh and blood, had had the wickedness and audacity to turn up on her doorstep while she was monster sitting, with a pack of banner-waving morons.

'GIVE US SOME GUNS!' screamed Asti, kicking the garden gate open, and stepping past the railings on to the pathway.

'GUNS!' surged the tide of monster-hating banners.

The instant the front gate swung open Nelly flew to the door.

'WHAT ARE YOU DOING?' she screamed, confronting her sister from the doorstep.

'THERE SHE IS!' screamed Asti, pointing up the path. 'AND THERE THEY ARE!' she spat, pointing at Nelly's knees with a downward jab of her banner.

Nelly lowered her eyes to find the worried faces of the Wattwatt children peering through her legs.

'I couldn't stop them,' said Craig, joining Nelly on the step.

'LOOK AT THE LITTLE FREAKS!' screeched

Asti. 'LOOK AT THEIR WONKY YELLOW FACES, LOOK AT THEIR FREAKY EYES!'

'DEATH DEATH DEATH DEATH DEATH!!!!!' chanted Natalie, stepping forward to fuel the hatred.

'WHAT DO WE WANT?'

'DEATH TO MONSTERS!' bayed the pack.

Nelly had had enough. She launched herself from the step with her fists flailing and her eyes burning with fury.

'I'll kill you!' she screamed, thundering down the path.

'You'll have to catch me first!' screamed Asti, turning tail, hurling her banner at the railings and fleeing across the road.

Nelly hurtled after her, burst through the gate, hurtled through the sea of banners and jackknifed high into the air across the bonnet of an oncoming car. With a screech of burning rubber and sickening intake of breath, Nelly hit the tarmac of the road.

A moment followed. An awful, impotent moment.

No one moved.

No one breathed.

Slowly, the fingers of the braking car driver released themselves from the wheel. Slowly, the hands of the protesters dropped their protest banners to the ground. Slowly, the Wattwatt children turned their eyes from the road to Craig.

'NELLLLLLYYYYYYYYY!!!!!!' screamed Asti, sprinting back across the road, and dropping to her knees beside her sister.

Nelly's body lay lifeless in the road.

'DON'T TOUCH HER!' screamed Craig, springing from the doorstep. 'Whatever you do, you mustn't touch her.'

'SHE'S NOT MOVING!' screamed Asti hysterically. 'SHE'S NOT BREATHING!' she sobbed.

'I wasn't going fast,' whispered the driver, staggering from his car, pale with shock and fear. 'Twenty, twenty-five miles an hour, no more, I've only just pulled away from my house. I just didn't see her. She just ran out in front of me. I COULDN'T STOP!' he trembled.

But no one was listening. The lumps in everyone's throats were for Nelly.

Craig dropped anxiously to Nelly's side, and crouched beside Asti. Nelly's body was there, but her spark was gone. Her eyes were closed, and her smile was shattered.

'She's dead,' sobbed Asti. 'I've killed my own sister!'

'SOMEONE RING AN AMBULANCE!'

screamed Craig, glaring at the group of girls that had frozen by the gate.

Hands slipped into pockets, and nines after nines after nines were guiltily punched.

'Oh no!' said Craig, thumping the road with his fist. 'The ambulances are on strike!'

Asti crumpled into a sobbing heap beside Nelly's lifeless body.

'IT'S ALL MY FAULT!' she screamed. 'IT'S ALL MY OWN STUPID FAULT!'

'We'll have to move her,' said Craig, slipping his arm under Nelly's shoulder, and easing her head up from the road. 'You're going to have to take her to the hospital in your car!' he shouted to the driver.

The driver of the car stood shaking beside the front bumper. 'I was only doing twenty or twenty-five, I promise,' he said in a haze of deepening shock.

'Look, either you take her, OR I CARRY HER!' screamed Craig, trying to bully some sense into him.

Craig wrenched a rubber glove from his hand

and pressed the flat of his palm against Nelly's cheek.

'Oh, God no,' he thought. Her face was cold and turning blue.

'NOOOOOOOOOOOOOOOOOOOOOO!!!!!!' he screamed, tears bursting from his cheeks.

'Stand back! lay her down, what what!' crackled a voice of calm authority.

Craig looked up to find the zigzagged faces of Wak and Zap striding from the kerb towards him.

'What happened?' crackled Wak. 'Quick, tell me what has happened!'

'She's been hit by a car.' Craig shook, too gutted to explain any more.

That was all that Wak needed to know. With multiple twists of his ears, he lowered his zigzagged head to Nelly's chest and listened.

'Her heart's stopped!' he crackled. 'Stand back!'

Craig wrapped his arms around Asti's sobbing figure and gently pulled her to the kerbside. What little hope there was lay with Wak now. There was nothing anyone else could do.

All eyes dropped to road level as Wak and Zap

crouched either side of Nelly's body and made final adjustments to their ears.

Wak leaned over Nelly's body and placed both of his palms firmly on to her chest.

'THUMP' went his palms, jolting Nelly's chest upwards from the road with the force of an electrical resuscitator.

Nelly's shoulders dropped back on to the tarmac, and her cheek fell lifelessly to one side.

Zap took over immediately, turning her left ear a fraction clockwise, and then attaching her palms firmly to Nelly's chest.

'THUMP!' went her palms, slump went Nelly's shoulders, and then 'grooaaaannn', the softest of sounds issued from Nelly's lips.

'She's breathing again,' crackled Zap, rising from the tarmac and leading his wife through the bannerless crowd of girls that were still frozen by the gate. 'Are you OK, children?' he crackled protectively.

Asti sprang from Craig's side and swooped like a tearful eagle on to Nelly's chest.

'I'm so sorry, Nelly, I'm so so sorry. I hate

myself for what I've done to you, I really do,' she sobbed. 'I'm horrible, I'm hateful, I wish I was dead, I just don't deserve to have a sister like you. I wish I was like you, Nelly, I really do, you're so funny and clever, and cool and everything, and I'm just a spiteful hateful cow! I hate myself, I loathe myself and I don't blame you for hating me too. I don't really hate monsters,' she sobbed, 'I just hate them because you like them, that's all. I don't really want them to die, I just want ME to die. Everyone would be better off without me!'

Nelly's eyes opened weakly and a warm smile broke across her face.

'Darren Leadbetter wouldn't,' she smiled.

Asti plunged her knuckles into her eye sockets and wiped as many of her own tears away as she could.

'Darren Leadbetter fancies you rotten,' Nelly whispered softly.

Asti's eyes welled up again and her fingers reached forward to tenderly stroke Nelly's hair.

'I don't care about Darren, I don't care about nose studs or tongue studs or belly-button piercings or crispbreads or make-up . . .'

'Make-up!' gasped Nelly, a little unconvinced.

'OK, I still care about make-up,' sobbed Asti 'but I'd give them all up for you.'

'And I'd give up my sardine T-shirt and my scrunchy for you,' whispered Nelly, puckering her lips mischievously for a kiss.

'Me first!' said Craig, diving forward to steal the first kiss of their first date.

'Me next!' laughed Asti, dropping down to plant a smackeroony.

'That's cherry blush lipstick,' she smiled. 'It's really expensive but you can borrow it if you like!'

'Maybe I will!' winced Nelly, inching her shoulders stiffly up from the road.

'Do you feel OK?' asked Craig. 'Nothing broken?'

'A bit bruised,' said Nelly, slowly sitting herself up. 'But no, nothing broken.'

The three friends looked back towards the Wattwatts' house. Protest banners lay scattered across the pavement like giant jack straws. Natalie and the rest of the girls had sloped away, opting for no payment and a very long walk home.

The car driver was sitting on the pavement now, beside his car, still wrestling with the after-effects of deep shock.

Zap, Wak and the children were waiting patiently on the doorstep.

'Come and meet the Wattwatts,' said Nelly, as Craig and Asti helped her to her feet.

'I'm going to give them a huge hug!' smiled Asti.

'I wouldn't do that if I was you,' laughed Craig, 'or you'll be needing an ambulance next.'

'Save it for Darren Leadbetter!' smiled Nelly.

Asti stepped through the gate of the Wattwatts' home and toe-poked the banner she had lobbed at the fence.

'Is it true?' she said. 'Does Darren really fancy me?'

'Yup,' said Craig, 'he told me himself.'

'Why didn't you tell me?' asked Asti.

'You know why,' sighed Nelly.

Asti nodded ruefully, and slipped her fingers into her sister's hand.

'I've got something to tell you.' Asti smiled.

'Oh yes?' said Nelly, smiling back at her twin.

'You had another phone call from some monsters this afternoon, just after you left the house. They were called Flitts, and they want you to monster sit for them too . . .'

'Cool,' smiled Nelly.

'In Cornwall!' smiled Asti.

Nelly stopped dead in her tracks.

'Cornwall?' she gasped. 'That's the other end of the country! How did they hear about me in Cornwall!'

'Sounds like news of Nelly the Monster Sitter is spreading far and wide!' chuckled Craig.

'Nelly and the Monster Sitter*S*!' smiled Nelly. 'From now on, if it's OK with you, Nelly's monster sitting service is going to expand its services!'

'How do you mean?' asked Asti.

Nelly placed her arms around the shoulders of Asti and Craig, and gave them both an excited squeeze.

'From now on,' she beamed, 'there's going to be THREE OF US!'